E.S.C.A.P.E.(Eventually Sex Cripples A Persons Emotions)

Im Him

Published by Im Him, 2023.

This is a work of fiction. Similarities to real people, places, or events are entirely coincidental.

E.S.C.A.P.E.(EVENTUALLY SEX CRIPPLES A PERSONS EMOTIONS)

First edition. October 21, 2023.

ISBN: 979-8223539834

Written by Im Him.

Table of Contents

E.S.C.A.P.E. 1

WAKEY WAKEY 2

K.I.M. | ADDICTED 9

Show Me The Proof 10

The Interrogation 51

1993 | Biggs N Duce 54

Interrogation continued 62

I Thought I Lost You 68

I Thought I Lost You | let Monique tell it 78

The Recovery 91

Three Days Later 96

17 Years Ago 102

Three Days Later | continued 111

I'm Sure It Wasn't Him | L.A.'s back 113

Trigga Trigga 127

Later That Day 139

I'm Sure It Wasn't Him | Continued 148

This Means War!! 151

5 Days Later 155

Kill or Be Killed 161

Long Kiss Good-Night 190

33 Days Later 197

MEANWHILE....... | Bitch You Mad or Nah? 203

Back At Janel's Place 210

Like You'll Never See Me Again 215

Time Is Of The Essence 221

THE END 228

E.S.C.A.P.E. | Eventually Sex will Cripple A Person's Emotions 229

~~(Eventually Sex will Cripple A Person's Emotions)~~

Love has potential to be the best thing that has ever happened to

you, in that same

breath can become your worst nightmare. Only when the love starts to become toxic does the
relationship begin to spiral downhill. True, when you love someone, you don't just give up when
the going gets tough, but when you don't know when to cut your losses and walk away, then
you become trapped in an unhealthy relationship. The one thing that holds 1 out of every 3
relationships together is sex. The relationship was built off physical chemistry. Sex
becomes the only aspect of the relationship you both enjoy. Well, what about the toxic
relationships that aren't bound together by sex? Have you ever held ya breath against
someone and when you started to gasp for air you held it in a little longer, because you didn't want to be the first one to give up?... Well, that's the same resistance to being the first one to give in. It's the same reason why a lot of people are stuck in toxic relationships today. When you love someone, sometimes it's hard to let go, but you must for your best interest. At the end of the day, your happiness is key, so you have to pull away.... "But what happens when it's too late to ESCAPE?"

(Chapter 1)

"L.A........... L.A......." I heard a voice call out. "Wake ya bitch ass up," the voice yelled out as a

burst of cold water splashed across my face. When I went to wipe my face, I noticed that my

wrists were shackled together and connected to a knotted rope.

"Where am I?!" I yelled out, "Who are you?!" I followed up as the voice in the darkness let out

a chuckle.

"You can yell as loud as you want L.A. no-one's going to hear you," the deep voice

responded. I couldn't help but to think how familiar that voice sounded and then it hit me. But

it couldn't be.

"Bossman?" I asked before I began to hear clapping.

"Ding, Ding, Ding we have a winner," he responded as the lights came on. I looked at him

standing in the doorway with half of his face badly burned.

"But........ But how.......how...... how is this possible?" I said sitting there speechless, trying to

piece together words. He didn't even attempt to offer any response. There was just a moment

of silence, then I heard a thump, "What was that!?" I asked. Bossman just looked and smiled.

"Well, I'm not one to ruin surprises but I have someone here that seems eager to see you, sit

tight," he said as he walked out of the room. I couldn't figure out why or how Bossman was still

alive, but I damn sure wasn't trying to stick around to see what it was that he wanted from me. It took me a few tries, but I finally made it to my feet and attempted to dash toward the door. I

was swept off my feet and onto my ass by the rope that connected my shackles together,

which seems to have been attached to a steel beam on the ceiling, where I was seated. A stiff

pain shot up my back from the fall, as I rolled over onto my side.

"Well, well, well L.A. I have to say I always knew you weren't the brightest candle on the cake,

but I figured you would be smart enough to know that I wouldn't dare leave you alone in a room.

Unchained with the door to ya freedom wide open," he explained, before I felt his boot damn

near penetrating my side. He then grabbed the other end of the rope, which hung in front of the

light switch and pulled down on it. The more he pulled the further back the rope pulled me until I

was right back where I started. Bossman didn't stop pulling on that rope until I hung about 3

feet off the ground. He reached into the hallway and dragged in someone sitting in a chair. I

couldn't make out who it was because their face was covered.

"Bossman .... What do you want, man? Why are you doing this?" I asked, but again he didn't

offer a response. "Bossman!" I called out and he still didn't respond. He only continued to tie

up the legs of the person sitting in the chair. "James! You son of a bitch, you hear me fucking

talking to you!? Answer me!!" I protested out of pure frustration. I watched as he removed the

cloth from the head of the individual sitting in the chair and right then my heart sank to my feet.

"Oh, I didn't know we were on first name bases Frank, what's wrong, cat got ya tongue?"

Bossman said as he let out a light snicker. Tears began to run down my face as I spoke.

"Mama?" I said in more of a question like manner, before he grabbed her by her hair lifting her

head up. "James, what is it that you want....... whatever it is you don't have to involve her," I

added, damn near pleading for his mercy. Trying to convince myself that he might have a

heart and would let her go. "Oh... so you are capable of using your inside voice?" he said

sarcastically as he continued. "Well L.A. now that I have your attention, I feel a little more

inclined to answer a few of your questions. But choose wisely, you only get 3."Bossman said

as he rolled over a small table and stationed it on the side of my mother. From where I was

hanging, I couldn't really see what it was that was on the small table. I could see my mother

begin to panic when she glanced over.

"What the hell is that?!" I asked. Bossman rolled the table over to the other side of my mother,

where nothing was obstructing my view. I then saw what it was that my mother was freaking out

about. And slowly but surely, I began to get a frog in my throat as he responded.

"Oh this? These are just a few tools I plan on using." And with that comment, frustration

immediately started to set in.

"Use on who?!" I asked before looking down at the sea saw, hammer, scalpel, and a grill lighter
that laid across the table.
"Your mother," he responded with deadly conviction.... There was a slight moment of silence.
Then he continued, "I actually have the easy job here, it's you that has to make the difficult
decision. You must choose how she will die," he finished.
"You son of a bitch!" I shouted as I began squirming back and forth trying to shake loose. "Why
can't you..." I started to say before being quickly cut off.
" Ah, ah, ah....... if I was you, I would be careful with the next question that comes out of ya
mouth, because it will be your last," Bossman said.
"What?! Wait, you said I got three!" I protested.
"Exactly, and you've already wasted two," He swiftly responded. In that moment everything
slowed down and I felt my lips begin to move yet I had no idea of what was making its way out.
"Why.... why are you doing this?" I asked as I felt a tear run down my cheek.
"Why am I doing this? Did you really just ask me that ridiculous ass question? Well, if it
hasn't kicked in by now, then I guess it's only right to tell you, he said as he went to lay my
mother on the floor. He walked over to a similar makeshift contraption that I was hooked up to,
only this one was connected to her legs. He continued speaking as he pulled down on the rope,
elevating my mother higher and higher off the ground.
"You stripped everything from me.... EVERYTHING! My mother, my father, my sister, and

my girl and yet you honestly thought that wouldn't come back and bite you in ya ass?"

Bossman asked posing a rhetorical question as he reached for the scalpel on the table then

continued.

"Mama E, is there anything you would like to say to your son?" he asked as he removed a

piece of cloth from her mouth....

" Son... I love you-" she said as tears trembled from her eyelids. She continued, " I want

you to take...." Everything slowed down and her voice died off as I watched Bossman run the

scalpel clean across her jugular vein.

"I love you too mama," I softly muttered as I closed my eyes.

"Hold ya head up L.A., it will be over in a moment. And maybe then you'll see how it feels to

have nothing, to lose everything!" he said as he made his way over to me. I watched until

my mother hung there lifelessly before the rage began to set in. "Is that realization of

emptiness starting to set in yet?" he asked with a grin on his face.

"You self-centered piece of shit, do what you're going to do to me, but you better make damn

sure, you kill me because I have every intention of killing you," I said, spitting in his face. He

placed the scalpel to my neck as he spoke.

"Bad news .... you can't kill what's already dead!"

I woke up panting. That dream gave me a banging headache.

When I opened my eyes, all I saw was darkness! To make matters worse when I attempted to

reach for my face, I realized that both my ankles and wrist were bound to a chair. I tried to move the chair but failed miserably. The damn thing was bolted to the floor! I have on

nothing but my boxers and socks. I am beginning to worry! I don't know where I am

or how I got here. I tried my hardest to get my hands free, but I couldn't. Whatever bondage this

is, it was done very tightly. Literally moments after I gave up on freeing up my hands, I hear the

sound of heels coming from behind me. Then a door opened at my 6 O'clock. Just enough

light from the hall entered the room allowing my vision to no longer be impaired.

"Hello...? Who's there?!" I asked but silence was the only thing I heard. I know there's

someone there. Answer me DAMNIT!" I added. Even though there was a little light in the

room, I was still unable to turn my head enough to see who was behind me.

" Well, I'm glad to see that you're awake now," the familiar voice said in a soft tone. I started to

hear a combination of rusted wheels and high heels getting closer. The squeaking of the rusted

wheels came from an old utensil table that dentist would use to hold the tools to clean your

teeth. The table had a cloth over it, but I can tell by the impressions that there is something

underneath. I started to smell the fragrance of a woman. The closer the sound of the heels got.

"Who are you? Where in the hell am I?" I asked but there was no response, only the sound

of heels. The heel clicker finally made its way into my line of sight. The only angle I got at first

was from behind. She stood there in a pink laced panty and bra set with a pair of pink and
black Jordan heels. There was only one other woman I have ever seen that fit on......
"Janel?!" I asked. She spun around with a grin on her face.
"I figured you would know who it was from behind," she said as she made her way over to me,
climbing on top of me before continuing. "Besides, that's really the only angle you've been
seeing me from for the past few months," she added in a soft tone close to a whisper in my ear.
As she ran her tongue down the side of my neck, she started kissing me all over my neck and
chest. I felt her hand sliding into my boxers grabbing my dick.
"Janel .... I told you that I was done," I said...
"Well L.A. if that's how you feel... she said pausing as she reached over to remove the cloth
from the table. There lay a knife, gun, and a meat cleaver. She grabbed the gun and shoved
the barrel right down my boxers as she continued, "I might as well kill you now."
For you to understand how we got to this point. I have to take you back to a few
months ago....

ADDICTED

Your love is like a drug that I just can't get enough of, so I guess I'm addicted.

They say love is war and war is love. No one said it would be a picnic but loving you is worth so

much more than every woman I've been with.

See we both have our separate issues, you know shit we have to deal with,

Battle wounds and broken hearts that type of pain kills shit but through it all we found each other

and baby that's real shit.

See you're the woman that I want to spend the rest of my life with.... bite lips,

Rough sex in the morning... light kiss, then turn around and be the same woman I make love all

night with

But it's not about the sex though... Don't get me wrong I'ma nympho,

But making you climax ain't the only thing I'm in foe....

And you can attest to that I mean just look how far we've made it,

Just kissing, barely touching, no oral or penetration never once did I propose or entertain the

conversation so without a doubt my love for you is genuine and your heart right now is the only

thing that I'm penetrating.

I don't do this often because my words can get twisted, see here she goes again enticing

me with this drug knowing that I'm addicted.......

Opening my eyes, I can't help but to thank God for blessing me with

another day, and

waking up to my beautiful fiancé is a major bonus... Look at her, just lying there with nothing

but a sheet halfway covering her body. See we have a "No Clothes Policy," just in case of days

such as this one where clothing would just get in the way. I slowly rolled her over onto her back.

Making sure I don't wake her up, once I remove the sheet I just sit there for a moment and

admire her temple. I pull her down to the edge of the bed and kneel to one knee as I

spread her legs placing them on my shoulders. I start softly kissing her inner thighs.

She's still sleeping, but clearly her body is awakening. Because the closer I get to her pussy the

wetter she gets. I slowly and softly run my tongue up and down between the lips of her

pussy, to first please my taste buds. Then I go in for the kill. I wrap my hands around her thighs,

and go to work. Moments later I hear her begin to moan and I feel her fingers roaming

through my hair.

"Mmmmmhh... baby what are you doing?" she asked.

"Shhhh..." I simply responded as I reached up wrapping my hands around her neck. "Relax," I

added in a soft tone as I continued to play with her clit with my tongue. After a few moments, I
feel her thigh muscles tighten up and her back arch; and her moans are sounding more and
more soothing. She grabbed me by my hair and pulled me up to eye level. It seems like she's
ready. She wrapped her arms and legs around me, twisting her body with a swift
maneuver she was on top of me.
"You know I don't like being woken up out of my sleep, right?" she asked as she reached down
and began stroking my dick.
"Yeah, I know! I knew you would like this wake-up call," I said as I watched her softly kiss me
all over my body while slowly working her way down.
"Mmmmmh ... is that right?? Well maybe I could get use to this," she said as her soft warm lips
kissed the head of my dick. I watched as she kept making it disappear but before she could
finish, I had to stop her. This morning isn't about me, so I pulled her up to eye level then eased
my dick into her warm, tight, wet pussy. We both let out a moan of satisfaction. I watched
as she placed her hands on my chest, she started rocking back and forth. Her nails dug
deeper into my skin and her eyes began to roll to the back of her head.
"Oooooo.... daddy I'm about to cum!" she yelled as I felt her pussy muscles tighten. I leaned
forward encasing my arms around her body forcing her to take every inch with no motion.
Feeling my dick thrusting inside of her sent her into a bliss! As she reached her peak, she tried

to run but I wouldn't allow her to. With my grip firmly around her waist, she settled for just

sinking her teeth into my shoulder as she came. Both out of breath I softly whispered in her ear,

"Do you want to have my baby?" The question shocked me more than it seemed to bother

her. She placed her hands on my chest, easing me to my back, laying on top of me and

whispered, "I can't wait to have your child," she said. Realistically, I'm not ready for a child but

everything with her feels so right and I know with her by my side anything is possible. While

on top of me and my dick deep inside of her, she turns around and begins slowly leaning

Forward then throwing herself back. It's sending me into hyperdrive watching the lips of her

pussy wrap around my dick, so tightly and turning it into a whiteout. I let her take control and

do her thang for awhile and in doing so she was able to bust a few more times before the

finale. When I was ready to reach my boiling point, I laid her flat on her stomach and I climbed

on top of her. I ran the tip of my dick up and down the lips of her warm, soaking wet pussy

before ramming every inch of me into her. I watched as she gripped the bed and sheets with

one hand and with the other hand she held the pillow that she was screaming into. As I felt

myself about to pop, I take a fist full of her hair and yank it, pulling her face from the pillow.

"Ooooooo Shit!" Monique yelled. Letting out a loud moan as I threw this dick as deep as

Possible inside of her. And just like firecrackers we both popped. It was like her soul had been

touched the way her back arched downward into the bed. I rolled over and she climbed on top

of me laying her head on my chest.

"I love you Monique," I said as I fondled her hair.

"I love you too, Baby," Monique responded, gazing into my eyes. "I'm about to go get in the

shower," she added as she climbed off of me.

"Okay baby, what do you want for breakfast?" I asked as I sat up. She pushed me back down

To my back.

" No, you always cook for me! Let me shower then I'll make Bigg Daddy some breakfast," she

protested followed by a soft kiss on the cheek.

"You, cook for me?" I said with a bit of a snicker.

"Yeah L.A. I can cook," she responded with her hands on her hips.

" I'm cool with that," I said, smacking her on her ass as I went on. "Maybe I should wake you up

like this more often." Monique turned her head back toward me as she walked away.

"Whateva punk!" she said, trying to hold back her smile. I laid there in the bed for a moment,

trying to calm myself down from all the excitement that just transpired. After a moment or two,

I went ahead and made the bed with fresh bed sheets. Cleaned up the mess in the room

from the wild night before. By the time I was done cleaning up, I had lost track of time, but the

aroma of bacon in the air brought me back to reality. I made my way to the kitchen, there she stood at the island in the middle of the kitchen with nothing but a pair of ocean blue lace

panties. Her body glistening from her natural beauty and a little help from the skylight above

her, she stood there cutting up some fruit.

"What'chu making?" I asked as I snuck up wrapping her up from behind.

"Your favorite," she said, reaching her arm back softly caressing the side of my face. As I'm

kissing her on her neck, she uses her other hand to feed me a strawberry. "Strawberry

pancakes, bacon, eggs, with a small side of hash browns," she added. After taking a bite of

that strawberry, I whispered into her ear

"Ready for round 2?" I quickly followed the question up with slowly caressing the lips of

her warm, juicy pussy with my fingers. Sucking all over her neck while firmly gripping her

breast.

" Yesss..." she softly moaned out as she reached back pulling her panties to the side guiding

my dick into her tight pussy. I took my left hand and gripped the back of her neck bending her

across the granite countertop. With her face sideways and planted on the countertop I had only

made it halfway inside of her before noticing that she had already begun creaming all over my

dick.

"Well, maybe later...." I said in a soft tone with a smile on my face as I slowly pulled out.

"Why would you do that?!" she asked as she turned around and softly hit me across my chest.

"Awww...." I simply responded as I reached in to pinch her cheeks...

"That's not nice L.A." Monique said slapping my hands down then turning back around to

continue cutting up fruit.

"Nah... you know Bigg Daddy likes to play the tease game," I said as I gripped her waist.

"Yeah, yeah whatever..... go get in the shower or something," she said, waving me off.

"I love you Mo Mo," I said, kissing her shoulder and spanking her ass as I walked away.

"Mmhhmm ... love you too punk!" Monique mumbled. So as planned I hopped in the shower,

Doing my little one two. I'm standing there just letting the hot water run down my body. I

couldn't help but to think about my life. Thinking about how if I had not gone through the

struggles that I went through I wouldn't be the man I am today. I have lost a lot of loved ones

throughout my time, but Monique and my mother which are the two most important people in

my life that are still in my life. And I'll be damned if I allow anyone to change that. As I got out

of the shower, I started brushing my teeth. I hear a phone ringing in the distance. It couldn't

have been mine, my phone is on vibrate and the house phone doesn't have that ringer, so I

assumed it was Monique's. The ringing eventually stopped, and I continued brushing my teeth.

Not even a full minute later, I hear glass shattering and a loud screech coming from the kitchen.

I expeditiously wrapped a towel around my waist and ran towards the cries of agony. When I

made it to the threshold of the kitchen, I saw glass from what looked to be a coffee mug broken

into all different shapes and sizes on the floor. Instinctively, I became a little worried that

Monique may have hurt herself. I make my way around the glass shattered on the floor and

there she is sitting in the corner erupting in tears.

"Baby??? Baby??? Hey, what's wrong?" I asked as I kneeled to one knee embracing her.

"Why God? Why me...?!" Monique said as she tried to propel me away...

"Look at me. LOOK AT ME! " I hollered as I shook her by her shoulders. "Mo Mo, what is

it?" I added.

"James'........ James is DEAD!!!" she struggled to say before burying her head into my chest.

"What? Hey, hey, hey relax honey.... take deep breaths .... how did he die?" I asked despite,

already knowing the answer.

"I.... I'm not sure. My mother just called me and told me that he was dead and that she

wanted me to meet her downtown at the Coroner's Office to identify his body."

"Okay, how is your mother taking it?" I asked, as the question slipped out, I knew that it was by

far the most idiotic question I could have asked.

"She's a mother who just lost her oldest child, which just so happens to be her only son L.A. so

how do you think she's taking it?!" Monique said with heavy indignation in her voice.

"You're right Baby Girl, that was a very dumb question for me to have asked," I said as I wrapped my arms around her helping her to her feet. "Come on, let's get dressed and make our way down there," I finished. She shook her head in acceptance and we rapidly made our way to the room got dressed and went out the door. The whole ride downtown she's just sitting in the

passenger seat silent and continuously wiping tears from her soft cheeks. I couldn't help but

to think to myself, "How were they able to identify the body so quickly?" Shit in cases like

this, it usually takes four weeks, maybe even longer to positively identify a body. I didn't have

much time to analyze every possibility before pulling up to the Coroner's Office.

"Listen honey it looks like your mother is already here. I know that this is hard on you as well

but right now, you need to be strong for her," I said as I leaned over to kiss her forehead. She

just shook her head in acknowledgment that what I said was right. She then waited for me to

open her door. Monique and I walked into the Coroner's Office and instantly Monique saw her

mother in the corner of the room off to the left, sitting in the fetal position crying.

"Mama!" Monique called out as she ran over to her mother's side. I was not too far behind

her. "Mama, what did they say? Has anybody been out here to speak with you?"

"A detective came and spoke with me. I told him to hold off on telling me anything until you

were here. I'll let him know you're here now," she said in a weeping voice.

" Nah, Mama Mason, you stay put I'll go let them know," I said making my way towards the
front desk.

"His name is Detective Davis," Mama Mason called out.

"Hi sweetheart, how are you?" I asked the young lady at the desk.

"I'm fine, and yourself sir?" she responded.

"I've actually had better days as you can imagine. Could you please inform Detective Davis
that the Mason family is ready to see him now," I questioned. The young lady picked up the
phone and hit three numbers.

"Yes, Detective, the Mason family is ready to see you now. Okay," she said before hanging
up the phone and turning her attention to me "Sir? Detective Davis is on his way out."

"Thank you," I said as I turned and walked away.

"Oh, and sir? I'm sorry for your loss," she said, extending her condolences. Moments after
reconnecting with Monique and Mama Mason a dark skinned, mid aged man standing 6'3 and
weighing about 140+ pounds appeared.

"Hello again Detective Davis, this is my daughter, Monique," Mama Mason said.

"Hello Monique, I am Detective Davis. I am the lead Homicide Detective in your brother's
case," he said as he shook her hand.

"Homicide!?" Both Monique and Mama Mason called out almost simultaneously.

"Yes, your son, your brother along with another victim that we have yet to identify have been
Murdered," Detective Davis said.

"How!?" I asked

"I'm sorry and you are?" The detective asked as he looked at me with the side eye.

"A very close friend," I responded.

"Well, with all due respect if you're not blood to the victim then you don't need to be included in

this conversation," Detective Davis said.

"And with all due respect, blood couldn't make us any closer, so as far as I'm concerned, I am

family...Officer Davis!" I firmly stated.

"It's Detective Davis!" he protested.

"Yeah! Whateva! Same difference, y'all all a part of the swine family right!?" I replied.

"What did you just say to me son?" he said as he stepped closer towards me.

"Detective Davis!" Mama Mason called out grabbing his attention as she spoke, "This

young man has been a part of our lives for years! And if anyone was to ask me what his

relationship to this family is, I would tell them that he's, my son! So, with all due respect,

anything you have to say to my daughter and I, you can and will say it in front of him!" Mama

Mason finished. Even though I could tell by the look on his face that he still didn't want me

present he just complied with Mama Mason's request.

"As you wish Mrs. Mason. Now, if you all could please follow me." he said while opening up a

Door leading to the back of the office. Down the hall standing in front of another door in the

Hallway stood an older, white man with something like a lab coat on and glasses.

"Mrs. Mason this is Dr. Yacub, one of the top three medical examiners in the state," Detective
Davis said.
"Hello Mrs. Mason, it's both a pleasure and unfortunate to meet you," Dr. Yacub said as he
shook our hands.
"Same here Dr. where is my son?" Mama Mason asked.
Dr. Yacub looked over at Detective Davis. After Detective Davis nodded his head Dr.
Yacub began to speak, "I must warn you all that what you are about to see may be hard to
stomach," he said as he opened the door that he was standing in front of. It took my eyes a
moment or two to adjust to the bright lights. I think the first thing we all noticed was the steel
operating tables in the middle of the room with a white sheet over it. It's clear that by the way
it's protruding that something is underneath it. I looked over my shoulder and saw Monique
holding Mama Mason. As Mama Mason wiped tears from her eyes, "Is it really that bad Dr.
Yacub?" Monique asked.
"I'm afraid so," he answered as he pulled back the white sheet before going on. "Mrs. Mason,
Unfortunately, your son was burned beyond recognition. And because of these severe burns, I
was unable to obtain any blood samples".
"So how do you know this is my son!?" Mama Mason cried out abruptly interrupting Dr. Yacub.
He then opened the folder he had been holding and handed it to Mama Mason.

"Well luckily Mrs. Mason because of your son's prior juvenile record my team and I were able to

identify him by his dental record in our system." Detective Davis stepped in and said before his

phone rang, "I am sorry Mrs. Mason I have to take this" he added before he stepped away....

" Did he suffer?" Mama Mason asked Dr. Yacub.

" No! Mrs. Mason, if you will take a closer look here," he pointed at the abdomen of the severely

singed body "and here," he said pointing at the frontal lobe before continuing. "These entry

wounds here tell me that your son was shot in both his abdomen and his head before being lit

on fire," he said.

"Okay so if a gun was involved there must be some shell casings that were found at the crime

scene that could lead to who killed my brother!?" Monique stepped in and asked, in more of a

matter of fact kind of tone.

" And that typically would be the case," he said handing her a sheet of paper out of the folder

before continuing, "but the bullet fragments that I pulled from your brother's skull and abdomen

were not big enough to determine what type of gun was used and tested negative for any

prints. But in my expert opinion and taking into consideration the size of the entry and exit

wounds I would guess the weapon used was a Glock45," Dr. Yacub stated. I watched as Mama

Mason began to tear up and mourn, it was a painful sight to see but little did I know it was

About to get worse. Moments later Detective Davis re-entered the room with a unyielding look
on his face.
"Ah.... ah....... Mrs. Mason?" he said.
"Yes?" she answered, wiping away her tears.
"One of my field officers is on his way down here as we speak with the official documents.
Does the name, Richard Livingston, mean anything to you?" he asked.
"Yes," Mama Mason said, hesitant to answer.
"How do you know him Mrs. Mason if you don't mind me asking?" he said.
" He's my babies' father, both Monique's and James' dad. What does he have to do with my
son?" she asked with mild anger in her voice. Detective Davis placed one hand on his head
And the other on his hip as he spoke.
" Mrs. Mason, I am sorry to tell you this."
"Tell me what?!" she interrupted.
"The second victim that we found with your son turns out to be Mr. Livingston," He stated. As
He finished that sentence I could see Monique's knees began to buckle, so I rushed over to her
side. She had tried to stay strong and stable for her mother, but she couldn't take it anymore.
Dr. Yacub pulled over two chairs for Mama Mason and Monique to sit in, as I helped Mama
Mason and Monique from the floor to the chairs. I feel my phone vibrate. Standing behind
Monique and her mother I checked my phone and there's a text from an unknown number that
reads, "L.A. I know your secret, and I have evidence! I know you did it.
"The first thing that

popped into my head was who the hell is this, and once I saw that there were no prior

messages between us I began to worry. I leaned down and whispered into Monique's ear...

"Hey baby, I have to call my mother, it's an emergency. I'm going to step outside really quick,"

I said.

"Okay honey," she said, cradling her mother's head in her arms. I swiftly made my way to the

front steps outside of the building. Went to the unknown number and pressed the call button.

The phone rang three times before someone finally answered.

"Hello?" I called out.

"L.A., nice to hear from you," the reposeful spoken voice said. My mind was racing about a

thousand miles per second trying to match a voice with a name. Unable to put one and one

together I regretfully asked.

" Who is this?"...

" I think that this conversation would go a lot smoother in person. So, why don't you meet me

downtown at the park on Martin Luther King St. in let's say 20 minutes. Yeah?" Now because of

the consistency of the speaker's soft voice I quickly concluded that this was a

woman on the other side of my phone.

"Look lady, I don't know who you are or what you want. But I'm not meeting you anywhere.

Whatever you have to say can be said over the phone. It's as simple as that." I said in

frustration. The woman began to laugh. "What the fuck is so funny?!" I asked.

"The fact that you think that you're actually in a position to make any requests or demands,
When I'm the one who knows your little secret. I'm sure Monique wouldn't be so happy to hear
About," she said.
"First off, my fiancé knows everything there is to know about me. There are no secrets between
us! So, there is NOTHING that you could possibly say to her about me that she doesn't already
know. I'm hanging up know" I said in an inconsiderate manner....
"That's fine, I'm sure Monique and her mother would love to have closure in the murder of
James." The phone grew silent before she continued to go on. "Wha-Wha-Wha... what's
wrong L.A. cat got your tongue? Well now that I have your attention, I'm pretty sure I have your
cooperation as well. Now you only have thirteen minutes to meet me at the park, luckily for you
I know you aren't too far away," she added. I looked around but saw no one looking in my
direction.
" How do you know where I'm at?" I asked.
" Not important L.A. tick tock, tick tock," she said, taunting me with the fear of time expiring.
" How will I know who you are?" I inquired...
"Go to the park and sit on the bench adjacent from the children's playground and wait for my
call," the woman said before hanging up. I looked down at my watch and made my way to the
car and the whole time I'm thinking about what the worst possible outcome could be if I don't

make it to the set destination in the next eleven minutes. As I am driving, making my way to the

park, my mind is traveling a thousand miles per second focusing on everything and nothing all

At the same time. And just before I got sucked into that mental twilight zone my phone rings.

"Hey, Baby Girl! What's going on?" I asked.

"L.A. what's going on, is everything okay?" Monique asked.

"Nah, not really but it will be, I had to leave," I answered.

"Leave? And go where?" she questioned." To my mother's, and I'm not sure what's wrong she

just asked me to get to her house as soon as possible. I was just about to call you. Listen...

take your mother home and sit with her until I get there, okay?" I said as I pulled into the

Parking lot of the park. Glancing down at my watch, I arrived with just a little over four minutes

to spare.

"Yeah, I can do that honey. Will you be long?" she responded.

"I don't plan on being long honey. I'll text you when I am on my way, okay? I love you, "I

stated, as I got out of the car and walked across the football field.

"I love you too honey," Monique responded before I could hang up, I heard her shout..." Hey

Honey, wait!"

"Yeah, what's up bae?" I asked, growing slightly irritated.

"Detective Davis wants to speak with you," she added and before I could get another word out I

heard his voice.

"Hey L.A., Detective Davis here. Hey, listen I have already had the opportunity to talk to Mrs.

Mason and who I understand to be your fiancé and asked them a few questions. I was
wondering if you could come by my office today?" He spoke.
"Ah, I'm not too sure about today. I have a very busy schedule and on top of that, this
unexpected tragedy is a lot to take in," I responded.
"How about tomorrow?" He quickly shot back.
"We will have to see what tomorrow brings," I answered, trying not to sound so definitive. As
he responded, his voice got lower as if he stepped away from the phone.
" Well, I'm going to put it like this... today is Monday. If I don't see you between now and next
Monday, I'll have no choice but to assume that you know more about these two homicides than
you claim to know," he finished... No soon as I made it to the park bench, I hear a beep in my
ear from an incoming call.
" I hear you loud and clear Detective I'll be sure to clear my schedule but right now I have to
go!" I said before clicking over to the incoming call. " I'm here, where are you?" I asked
becoming more and more impatient.
" You see the restroom to your left?" she asked.
" Yeah, what about it?" I countered.
" Go into the ladies' room and lock the door behind you" she said before hanging up the phone
just as swiftly as she made the demand. I looked around a few times as I made my way to the
area making sure I wasn't being followed nor seen. I made my way into the women's restroom
and locked the door behind me as instructed. Moments later I hear the sound of heels clicking

against the hardwood floors.

"Janel?! The bitch on the phone, was you?!" I asked. she stood there in front of the mirror

above the sink with a grin on her face as she spoke.

" What's wrong L.A. you look like you just saw a ghost," she said as she untied her belt. It was

dangling around her abdomen and connected to a black trench coat. Once untied completely it

revealed a matching red velvet bra and panty set. She started to walk towards me.

"You can stop right there!" I demanded, but she continued to get closer. With my back up

against the door cornered, she placed her arms around my neck. I quickly grabbed her by her

arms and placed her on the wall next to the door. "STOP!" I said. We done been through this

already! Nothing will ever happen between us!" I protested.

"Shhhh," Janel simply said, placing her index finger across my lips before continuing. "I know

what you said L.A. But that was before today," she said as she pulled her phone from her bra,

then continued. "Before I had any leverage," she said, dangling her phone in front of me. I

snatched the phone from her hand and pressed play on the video image that was already

preloaded. The moment that video played it felt like my heart had stopped beating. There it

was, indisputable evidence of me shooting and burning the bodies of James and Duce just gift

wrapped.

"How did you get this?" I asked, visualizing my whole world crashing down on top of me. She stood on her tippy toes and softly spoke in my ear answering my question.

"I was there..." she said leaning back against the wall removing the trench coat and placing it

on the floor before going on. "See I was getting this weird vibe from James a few days prior

and I thought it might be because he was cheating. So that night when he left, I followed him."

she finished.

"Who else knows about this?!" I asked. She caressed my face as she spoke.

"No one L.A. and that's the beauty of it. It's just our little secret," she said as she began to

kneel in front of me. I grabbed her by her hair and yanked her back to her feet.

"So, if you saw what I was capable of doing to one of my closest friends, what makes you think

I wouldn't do the same to a Bitch I could give two fucks about?" I firmly stated as my grip

Around her neck grew tighter.

"Be.... because" she struggled to speak so I released my grip. "Because unfortunately for

you," she paused, gasping for air before going on. "That same video you just looked at is

programmed into my computer." Janel said.

" And that's supposed to scare me? You just made it simple, if I kill you, I'll have to destroy your

computer as well." I said and Janel just started to laugh.

"I'm afraid it's not that simple L.A. See if I go 48 hours without logging in to my computer that

video clip is pre-programmed to be sent to both Monique and the lead homicide on the case.

Detective Davis? I believe it is?" she said as she reached for my belt buckle.

" What do you want Janel?" I asked once more.

" Ah, see now that, that's the simplest part of this whole thing. I want everything. If I need

money you'll provide it, a car you'll buy it, and when I want some of this dick..." she paused and

reached into my pants grabbing my dick before continuing "I'll get it!" she finished. I felt my

pants fall to the floor and all I could think about was Monique. Janel dropped to her knees and

began sucking my dick. Now even though my dick began to have a mind of its own the thought

Of cheating on my soon to be wife was repulsive. Once Janel finished topping me off, she

Stood up and grabbed my wrist leading me over to the sink. She sat on top of the sink and

pulled me in closer to her wrapping her legs around me. I just stood there like a deer in

headlights as she took my dick and ran it between the lips of her warm, succulent pussy.

"Unacceptable..." She said relinquishing her grip on my dick.

" What do you mean unacceptable?" I asked in frustration.

" Listen, I am not at all forcing you to fuck me... you clearly have a choice, a sucky one but a

choice nonetheless... I want you to fuck me, nah make love to me like you would make love to

Monique.... but if you can't do that then you could always just leave..." Janel said with devilish

persuasion. I knew right at that moment that I couldn't just allow this blackmail to go on for too long, but until I figure out another solution. For now, I have to bite the bullet and do what I have

To do to keep her happy and quiet.

" So, you truly want me to lay pipe down like that?" I asked as I wrapped my hands around her

Waist.

" Mmmmhmmm, yesss," she moaned out. I slid her panties to the side and made my way inside

of her. She let out a semi loud moan of relief as our bodies merged. Janel unlatched

her legs from around my waist and placed them against my chest. I pulled her legs together

And rolled her to her side while still deep inside of her. Janel was already starting to cum, and

The sink ended up getting so wet that she started to slide off the edge of the sink. So instead of

repositioning her, I pulled her down and bent her over the sink and started ramming my dick

inside of her tight pussy.

" Oh my god..... yeesss... just like that," she yelled out. Moments later while unengaged in the

act, I looked down at my watch and realized that it has only been almost twenty minutes.

"Oh my god," I muttered under my breath, doing something that you really don't want to do for

twenty minutes felt like hours. Honestly, I was starting to get annoyed. I figured since she

was enjoying herself so much the only way I would be able to bring this dreadful encounter to a

quick end would be to make her tap out. I wrapped her hair around the palm of my hand, pulled and in that same fluent motion driving my dick inside of her pussy trying to touch her heart with

the tip of my dick. I looked up and caught her reflection in the mirror in front of us. She's damn

Near biting through her bottom lip, with her eyes closed squeezing her titties and softly

caressing her nipples as I dug off deeper and deeper inside of her.

" Ah.. ah... ah...... yessss... mmmhhmm ... cum inside me L.A." Janel moaned out. Mid stroke

I stopped immediately.

" What? No!" I called out as I started to pull out. She reached her arm back and placed her

hand on my lower side digging her nails into my lower back as she spoke,

" I don't believe you have much of a choice L.A. seeing as though you didn't notice that?" she

said out of breath pointing at the top left corner of the mirror.

" Notice what!?" I asked with frustration. Then as she pointed again, I noticed it. I looked over

My shoulder only to confirm what I had only hoped not to be true.

She slowly started rocking back and forth as she spoke,

"So you see L.A. unless you just want things to end with you and Monique, I asked you to cum

inside of me." Right above the door was a silver Sony camera that had a blinking red light, and I

can only assume it's been recording this whole time. She went on to say, "oh and don't worry,

I'll be sure to edit the audio since its shooting live to my email," she finished.

"So, what happens if you get pregnant? Or is that apart of you plan as well?" I asked.

"I don't see that happening seeing as though I am on birth control. Now I would really

appreciate it if you stopped with all the stalling and give me what I'm asking for," Janel said as

she bent back over to the sink smacking her own ass as she started throwing it back. After

About another five minutes and a few more nuts from Janel I realized that for this to come to

an end I'm going to have to make myself cum. In one fluent motion, I pulled out spent her

Around and as she wrapped her legs around me, I rammed my dick inside her tight, petite, and

extremely wet pussy. Her thighs clutched down around my waist as I began to passionately

pound on her walls. I closed my eyes and pictured making love to Monique and moments later I

start to feel myself getting ready to reach that popping point and instead of slowing up like I

typically would, I speed up.

" Ah..... L.A. yesss I'm about to cum!" she yelled out, little did she know I was about to as

well. She nutted first and as I watched her warm cum slide down my dick, I pulled her in close

to me, chest to chest; and as she bit down on my neck like a newborn vampire thirsty for blood

I dove inside of her as deep as I could and bust. "Ahhhh, yessss," she moaned out as her

legs began to teeter. I slowly pulled out watching as nut started seeping out of her and onto the

sink.

" Are we done here?" I asked as I watched her rub her fingers across and around the lips of her pussy then licked her fingers clean.

" Not just yet," Janel paused climbing down off of the sink before continuing. "Looks like I

have a bit of a mess to clean up," she added angling her eyes down at my dick which at this

point had both of our nut dripping from it.

" Nah, that's not necessary," I protested. When I attempted to pull up my pants, she stopped me.

" No, I insist," she said pushing me up against the side wall of one of the stalls then slowly

dropping to her knees. Although the idea of cheating on my soon to be wife wasn't a pleasant

one, this time I couldn't help but to watch her soft, warm, pink lips gently wrap around my dick.

She turned my white chocolate covered meat stick back to its original hazelnut complexion. If

you know what I mean, I fixed myself as I headed for the door.

" I look forward to doing this again sometime soon" Janel said with a smile on her face as she

fastened her bra.

" I'd rather not," I muttered under my breath

" Oh... L.A...." Janel called out as I opened the door.

"What Janel?" I responded irate!

" Give Monique and her mother my condolences, will you?" she said with a sneaky grin on her

face. I just ignored the comment and made my way out of the restroom and to my car... Once I

made it to my car I got in and just sat there for a few moments gathering my thoughts and

processing everything that had just happened. I pull off and make my way home to shower.

because there was no way in hell I was going to meet up with Monique and Mama Mason with

Janel's scent all over me. About three blocks away from my house my phone rings.

"Incoming Call from Wife Monique " the Bluetooth voice in the car announced,

" Answer! " I command.

"Hello?" Monique said.

" Hey honey, what's up?" I asked.

" Nothing much baby, I just wanted to check up on you. Is your mom okay?" she questioned.

" My mom? Oh yeah everything is fine now," I responded remembering that I did use my

Mother as an escape route.

" Okay, are you going down to speak with Detective Davis today?" Monique asked.

"Nah baby not today. He ain't got shit of importance to say to me, right now you are my focus.

So he can wait," I said affirmatively.

"So, you are still coming over to my mom's?" she probed.

"Yeah babygirl, I should be there in about an hour," I stated before her background started to

get progressively louder.

" Okay honey, I gotta go my aunt just got here. I'll see you when you get here baby, love you."

Monique said with no hesitation.

" I love you too," I raved. I pulled up to my house and I noticed someone sitting on my front

porch with their head down in their lap. Once I pulled into the driveway and hopped out it

became easier to make out who the person was that's loitering on my property.

"Jackie?" I said as I watched her head sprout up before going on. "What... what are you

doing here?" I asked. She quickly stood up and as she wrapped her arms around me, I noticed

that she had a few bruises on her neck and one below her right eye.

"I heard what happened to James are you okay?" she asked placing the palm of her hands on

my cheeks.

" Me? No yeah, I'm good... but what happened to you?!" I asked with my hand on her chin

turning her head to get a better assessment of the damage.

" It's nothing," Jackie said as she moved my hands and held her head down.

" That's not just nothing.... come on, come inside," I said as I unlocked the door before

continuing. "Did Cell bitch ass put his hands on you?!" I asked assertively.

" L.A. ... relax, it's not his fault. I shouldn't have went looking through his phone," she protested.

" I don't give a fuck what you did, that doesn't give him the right to put his hands on you. Wait?

How did you get here I didn't see any of ya cars out there?" I asked as I looked in my closet for

a fresh outfit to put on after I get out of the shower.

"He took the car keys and my phone, so I walked and that's why I didn't call before coming,"

Jackie said, as she sat on the corner of my bed. I stepped into the bathroom and left the door

cracked.

" What! He took your damn car! Where are the babies?" I asked as I stepped in the shower.

"I had my mom come and pick them up before I left," she stated and as she spoke her voice
was cracking as if she was crying.
" Did you call the police?" I yelled from the shower.
" No L.A.... I didn't. At the end of the day, he's still my husband" She argued. Now Jackie,
being the closest female friend that I have and the love that I have for her.... there is no way in
hell, I'm going to let anyone bring harm her way. Luckily for Cell today I don't have the time to
deal with the issue at hand but she knows just as well as I know that he will get dealt with. So, I
finished washing up and I rinsed off. I stepped out of the shower with my towel wrapped around
My waist and walked into my bedroom.
"True that's your husband, but at the end of the day you don't deserve to be mistreated and
abused," I said as I held her head up wiping the tears rolling down her cheeks before going on,
"if he won't treat you right, trust me there are plenty of men out there who would love to have
You by their side. Remember this, it's not true love if you find yourself settling and sacrificing
Your happiness for heartaches and headaches," I finished. Standing there in front of her with
Just a towel on and my body glistening cause of the steam from the shower, her eyes locked in
With mine.
"It's not a lot of good men left out here L.A." Jackie said as she continued to gaze into my eyes
and it felt like gravity was pulling us closer and closer together.

"Jackie.... I can't!" I said as I stopped like two inches away from her lips before going on. "I

know this isn't you, right now I know you're hurt and vulnerable so I would hate to feel like I am

taking advantage of you. I will always love you and be there for you. On top of that I'm

engaged to be married," I said as I turned away to get dressed.

" What...!?... Since when? And to who?" She said flabbergasted.

" Yeah, I proposed to James' sister, Monique, this past weekend and she said yes," I replied.

"OMG! Congratulations!" she yelled as she ran over to hug me before continuing, "I'm happy

for you. Whelp there goes another good man taken," Jackie added with a smile.

"I know right," I said as I laced up my kicks, threw on my jewelry, and put on my shirt before

continuing. "Hey, listen, I'm getting ready to swing by her mother's house and spend a little time

with her and the family, you wanna come? It will take ya mind off of a few things."

"Sure, I don't mind, but are you sure this is a good time? You know seeing as though she just

Lost her brother and all?" she asked curiously.

"Nah, it shouldn't be an issue, she needs all the support possible to stay strong for her

Mother," I answered as we made our way to the side door.

"You mean your soon to be Mother-In-Law," she stated jokingly.

"You know what I meant. So, are you coming, or no?" I asked as we stepped out onto the

porch.

"Sure, but I'm driving," she said as she pranced over to my car.

" Ha, driving what? Not my car young lady," I said, directing her over to the passenger side.

"Why can't I drive, I'm a good driver," Jackie said definitively.

"Oh really? I can't tell, " I responded as we both got into the car.

" Oh God L.A. really, are you still stuck on that? That was years ago," she said crossing her

arms over her chest.

"I didn't even have that car for a year, and you totaled it," I protested.

"Oh boy, I'ma need you to get over that," she replied punching me in the shoulder in a playful

manner.

" Oh! I'm over it! Ya ass just won't eva, eva.... EVA, eva, eva drive another one of my cars

again," I said as we both shared a moment of laughter, then as our drive began the

conversation that I had been dreading blew into existence.

" So.... what happened with Bossman?" she asked as she looked in the passenger mirror

fixing her makeup.

" Well, the detective on the case showed us the body this morning and James' body was

brutally burnt. The Medical Examiner says that the cause of death was a gunshot to both the

abdomen and head," I answered.

"Oh my god," She paused placing her hands in a triangle form over her mouth as she

continued. " So, he was murdered L.A.?" she asked as I saw her eyes begin to tear up. I shook

my head gracefully, "But who would want to kill James?" She asked baffled as she

continued," I mean I know he wasn't living the best type of lifestyle, but he was a good guy.

That's crazy" she professed.

" Yeah, tell me about it. But the crazier part is, whoever killed him killed his father as well. The

same way too. Shit the detective said they found them both in the trunk of his father's car," I

said.

"That was the story that was on the news like a week ago?" she asked still in disbelief.

"Yeah, that was them," I announced then the car just grew quiet for a moment before Jackie

finally spoke.

"Wow I can't even imagine how Monique must feel finding out that not only did she lose her

brother, but she also lost her dad as well," she said with the saddest look on her face We

pulled up to Monique's mother's house, the driveway was full, so I ended up having to park a

Few houses down. As I walked up to the house, I noticed a backyard full of what looks like

Monique's family.

" Hey Jackie listen, Monique and her mother need all of the support that we can possibly give

them. Even though this is a fucked-up situation for us all we can't allow them to give up on life

especially Mama Mason," I said as we walked up to the front door. Jackie said nothing in

response to my statement she just shook her head as if she understood what I was saying. I

rang the doorbell and Mama Mason answered.

"L.A. hey baby, Monique was expecting you a little later," Mama Mason said leaning in for a

hug.

"Yeah, I know, I finished up with my mom a little earlier so I came right over," I stated.

"Oh okay, well...." she paused moving me to the side before continuing, " who is this you got with you?" she asked sounding puzzled.

"Hey Mama Mason, it's me Jackie," she said stepping in a little closer as she continued, "It's been a while but we have met a few times before. Your son and I were good friends. I am so sorry for your loss," Jackie said as she extended her arms out for a hug.

"You do look familiar, honey, you can't mind me, my memory ain't what it used to be. But any friend of my son's is welcomed with open arms. Come, come," Mama Mason said grabbing the hand of Jackie and pulling her inside. When I stepped in, I saw people everywhere. A few I noticed and even the ones I didn't know I still spoke to them. Monique must have felt my presence in the room. Moments after entering the room I saw her come from the kitchen with an apron wrapped around her waist.

"Hey baby!" she said excited to see me as she came over and gave me a kiss. Then she turned her attention to Jackie.

"Monique, hey, I heard the good news. Congratulations on the engagement, but I am sorry for your loss," Jackie said.

"Jackie, right?" Monique asked.

"Yeah," Jackie quickly responded.

"Yeah, I remember my brother showing me some pictures of you and him at your wedding reception. So how did you get here?" Monique questioned with a hint of curiosity in her voice.

"Well, I rode with L.A." she answered.

"Yeah, honey after I left my mom's I just so happened to have swung by the house to change

And there she was sitting there on the front porch." I intervened.

"Hmm, just sitting there?" Monique asked with this strange look on her face. I already knew

what Monique was getting at with the statement posed as a question. When Monique and I

agreed to become a couple, I was very open and honest about my past. Jackie and I have had

A physical connection toward each other before. So, I felt that it was only right to let Monique

Know about Jackie, knowing that Jackie is still a part of my life even if she is only just a friend.

"Yeah, my husband and I got into it. He took a swing at me, and I left." Jackie explained.

Monique then eyed in on a few marks on both Jackie's neck and face.

"Cell.... Marcel did this?" Monique asked lightly, running her fingertips across the bruised areas.

"Yeah baby, but don't worry when I go to drop Jackie off at home this afternoon, I plan on

Having a "'Man to Man' convo with him," I said.

"I have already told him, Girl, that's not necessary," Jackie quickly stated.

"Yeah, baby do you really think it's a good idea to intervene with the issues in their marriage?"

Monique asked.

"Sweetheart, true it's their issues, their marriage. If it was you, you would want someone to

step in," I protested.

"True, I understand where you're coming from, but we both know you not stupid enough to put

ya hands on me like that, I think you enjoy having a penis." Monique said ending that statement

in a more subtle tone.

"Nah, Mama Watson brought him up better than that," Jackie said defending me as she nudged

her elbow into my side before continuing. "You got yourself one of the good ones girl," she

finished.

"Yeah, he's alright," Monique responded winking at me as she continued, "but anyways girl

are you hungry?" she asked.

"Yeah sure," Jackie responded.

"Alrighty follow me, hey baby go relax I'll bring you a plate," Monique said waving me away as

her and Jackie made their way into the kitchen.

" So, this is the young man you've been telling us about?" the elderly man asked.

"Hey how are you doing, Mr. Mason? It's a pleasure to meet you. Hopefully all of what you've

heard has been good," I said as I extended my hand out to shake his hand.

"I'm good son, considering the circumstances. Please call me Tom. This lovely lady here is

my wife," Tom said. I tried to give big Mama Mason a handshake, but she made it very

transparent that she was a hugger.

"It's a pleasure to meet you as well Mrs. Mason" I said.

"Honey, you're family, you can just call me Sharron. No Mrs. or Ms.... just Sharron." She

Declared before turning her attention to Monique and added, " I see you got yourself a looker

Mo Mo," Sharron said.

"Well, I'm not too worried about if he's a looker or not. My concern is ... does he treat you

right?" Tom questioned. Monique just nodded her head "yes" as she continued to show off

her engagement ring to her grandmother, Sharron.

"And I plan to continue doing so as well," I added.

"Good, now it has come to my attention L.A. that due to this untimely tragedy you weren't given

the opportunity to go about your proposal the traditional way," Tom said in a suggestive

manner.

"Dad stop it," Mama Mason said in a peaceful tone.

"No, no, no Mama Mason he's right. We are only getting married once and we might as well

do it right," I said before turning my attention back to Tom. "Mr. Mason.... I mean Tom, do I

have your blessings to marry your granddaughter," I asked. He pondered over the question as

if he really needed to think it over, and after a moment he spoke,

"Son.... you have my blessings," he said with aplomb. No sooner after we shook hands

and hugged it out when one of the ushers that worked for the funeral home approached us.

"I'm really sorry to interrupt, but the funeral director wants me to get everyone seated cause we

are just about ready to start. So, if you all could please take your seats it would be greatly

appreciated," the usher said.

"Not a problem" we all said simultaneously and moments after we took our seats a projection

screen dropped from the ceiling with a slide show filled with pictures of various moments in

Both James' and his father's lives. After about twenty minutes worth of slide show and another

Hour of idioms from various family members the pastor went up to the podium and said a few

Closing remarks.

"Ladies and gentlemen, I want you all to remember that we are gathered here today to

Celebrate LIFE not death, to remember these men as soldiers of God, not victims of these

streets. Can I get an Amen?" The pastor said.

"Amen!" everyone responded collectively.

"I didn't know Brother Livingston that well, but I know he did for his community. Now maybe he

didn't obtain the funds to do some of those things legally. But I know his heart was in the right

place. Now as for Brother James, a lot of you may have known him as "Bossman" or as a

troublemaker. I saw him as gifted. When Sister Mason first brought James to me as a

child, I said to myself this boy is going to need guidance. As we all do when we are of such

young age, even now. But I knew James would require much more guidance than some.

Many of you may not know this but James had dreams of being a sociologist. He wanted to be

able to help people with and through their issues. And it wasn't until he got older that he

allowed the streets to consume him. I know that today is not about me lord, but as a mentor, a
role model, a father figure to that young man I have failed him. Which means I have failed you
dear father. So, I ask today not just for forgiveness my lord, but James for yours as well. I
ask that you continue to be a guardian angel over your loved ones and help bring justice to the
ones responsible for your untimely death. Let us all join hands and offer a moment of silence
For the fallen soldiers here today." The pastor suggested as he bowed his head. The room
Went dead silent, no pun intended, you could damn near hear the heartbeats of everyone in the
room. After a few moments the pastor resumed his original upright position and gracefully
said, "Amen!" As the funeral came to an end, I happened to glance over to my left and there
stood Janel in the doorway, or at least it looked like her. When I went to do a double take, she
was gone.

"Okay ladies and gentlemen, I have just received confirmation that our food and refreshments
are ready for us next door," The funeral director said. Everyone began to lethargically move
From the funeral home over to the Swanson's Banquet Hall once the funeral was over.

"Hey baby you okay?" I asked Monique as we held hands exiting the building.

"Yeaaah, yea I'm okay," she responded with a lower spirit than what she came with.

"Hey, why did Mama Mason cremate the bodies before the funeral?" I asked remembering that

I only saw two urns on a table in front of the podium.

"It's something like an unspoken tradition. If two people die and their funerals are on the same

day, they must be cremated... if not then a third will die," she said in a stark tone.

"Sounds a little superstitious to me," I replied with my face a little twisted. Not in disbelief of

what Monique and her family has chosen to believe in, but at the fact that this bitch ass

detective had the audacity to show up to the funeral.

"Detective Davis hi.... odd seeing you here... did something new come up in the case?"

Monique questioned.

"Hey how you doing Monique? No, nothing just yet. I just wanted to come and pay my

respects. I knew your father," Detective Davis calmly said before turning his attention to me "

L.A.... glad to see you here, you know I was starting to think you had disappeared on me, but it

looks like you've just been avoiding me," The detective finished.

"Maybe I was.... or maybe I wasn't. Regardless this isn't the time nor the place for your bullshit

questionnaire," I quickly responded. The Detective quickly stepped to me within arm's reach.

Clearly invading my personal space, but once Monique saw me clench my fist she placed her

hand on the center of my chest and stepped between the Detective and me.

"Look Detective Davis, he's right, this isn't the time nor the place. I really do appreciate you for stopping by to show your respect. But I think you should leave now," Monique said in a calm yet

firm tone.

"You know what Monique you're right; I was out of line, and I think it is best that I go," he said

before turning his attention to me and continuing, "And you" he pointed," I got a feeling I'll be

seeing you real soon," he stated before walking away. I promise that the way I looked at the

man, if looks could kill he would have dropped dead right then and there.

"Hey.... hey, look at me," Monique demanded as she grabbed my chin angling my face down at

her. "Hey!... you know through thick and thin I got your back, but I need you to relax. Can you

do that for me?" she asked.

"Yeah ...I got chu," I responded, gazing into her eyes. I started to get this feeling that a day that

once started off on a positive note was quickly beginning to take a turn for the worst. We made

our way into the banquet hall and it was pure pulchritude. There was light music being played,

food and beverages including alcoholic ones being served. The atmosphere was just more

refreshing, and everything was going good for a while. Monique and I tasted a few appetizers

and had a few drinks. While we were conversing with some of her family and friends,

someone catches my attention.

"L.A.! Hey L.A." Jackie called out. Once Monique turned around, she instantly saw why I had

so much hate in my eyes.

"Hey... hey baby listen to me; I need you to keep a level head. Relax and play nice,"
Monique said, wrapping her arm around mine.
"Oh, my head is level. You should have just let me kill that little bitch when I had the chance,"
I responded.
"And how would going to visit my husband in jail and laying my brother to rest by myself
benefit anybody?" Monique asked in a low tone as Jackie approached us. Right in that
moment I knew that I mean just as much to Monique as she means to me.
"Hey y'all... how are you two doing?" Jackie asked hugging Monique and I before continuing. "
Monique, honey, the ceremony was beautiful. I still can't believe he's gone though," she added.
"Yeah, it was a beautiful ceremony, and I still can't believe he's gone either. I know that
he's still here with me in spirit," Monique responded. I wanted nothing more than to engage in
conversation with Jackie and Monique but I couldn't bring myself to take my focus off the little
bitch made ass punk that was making his way up behind Jackie.
" Oh, Cell, nice of you to make it," Monique said.
"Well, you know Bossman was my boy, so I had to come and pay my respects," Cell said.
"Ya boy, ha... you was cool with him because he hooked you up with free weed and blow... I
wouldn't call y'all boys... you were more like a leech if anything," I quickly said obtrusively.
" L.A. stop!" Monique quickly demanded.

"Nah Monique... L.A's right, comparing me and James' relationship to theirs, I guess I would

look like a leech... But is it because of the little bond James and I had? Is that really the reason

you look at me like a leech? Or is it because I got what you wanted first?" Cell asked as he

wrapped his arms around Jackie and kissed her shoulder.

"What the fuck did you just say to me?" I asked all roused up.

" L.A. he's been drinking a little too much today. Please don't pay him any mind... I'm sorry,"

Jackie stepped in and said as she pulled Cell away.

"Yeah, he told me all about you and my wife, and how you wanted her so badly back then. But

guess what, I got her!" Cell yelled out causing a scene.

"Cell, let's go right now! You're embarrassing me and showing your ass!" Jackie pleaded as

she tried to pull him back towards the door.

"Bitch, Move! You think I give a fuck about impressing these people," Cell said pushing Jackie

To the floor. As she fell, I saw her hit her head on the corner of one of the tables. It was like

everything was moving in slow motion, but once she hit the floor and I saw blood dripping from

her forehead I snapped. I ran over and tackled Cell to the floor and all you heard was "ooo's

And ahhhs" above us. Then I began to strike Cell in his face repeatedly. This time wasn't at all

like the last time. I wasn't allowing him to get a lick in. Family and friends tried to get me off him

But they were no match for my fury.

" Didn't I tell you..." (STRIKE) "The next time!" (STRIKE) "You put your hands on her!"

(STRIKE) " I....." (STRIKE) "Would kill you!" I shouted and as I looked into the eyes of his half-
beaten face, the room seemed to have gone silent and the only voice I could hear was
Monique's.
"Frank, baby please stop... he's not worth it please," she said as her voice faded away and the
noise level returned to normal and the next thing I knew, I was out.
(CREATE A BLANK PAGE FOR K.I.M. TO BE PUT IN LATER)

I was woken up to the smell of smoke being blown into my face and my head in

Excruciating pain.

"Ah Mr. Watson, glad you could join me... would you like a soda, coffee.... a cigarette?" the

voice said. I couldn't see anyone in my direct line of sight, but then again my eyes were still

adjusting to the bright lights in the room. When I opened my eyes, all I saw in the room was a

Big picture mirror flushed into the wall. I simply assumed that the mirror was one of those "one-

way" glass like they would use for a victim identifying someone out of a live line up. A table

sat in front of me bolted to the ground and a chair across from me aside from the one I was in

also completed the view of the room. "I don't think we no longer need these" the voice,

suggested as he removed the cuffs that I had just noticed was around my wrist. When I turned

around to see exactly who it was behind me; it came to no surprise when I laid my eyes on him.

"Detective Davis?!" I said with disgust.

"Yeah it is, my friend," he said, dropping a folder on the table in front of me before going on.

You know Frank, it's okay if I call you Frank, right?" he asked sarcastically as he continued. "

You know after reading your file it feels like I know you better and from the moment I laid eyes

on you I knew you reminded me of someone, I just couldn't put my finger on it until now,"

Detective Davis said as he sat down smoking his cigarette...

"I'm not sure what type of freaky fantasies you're into but I don't swing that way sorry." I said

with a straight face. The Detective let out a small chuckle before speaking,

"See even you got his same smartass sense of humor," he said offering me a cigarette before

going on. "Do you remember much about your father?" he asked. My eyes widen and anger

spiked at the idea of him even mentioning my father.

"What the fuck does my father have to do with any of this," I questioned in a wrathful tone.

"Well, while you were taking yourself a little nap, I ran your prints through our database and

that's how I found your file. Then I did a little digging, and I composed a theory that I believe

Ties you to the murder or both James Mason and his father, Richard. Care to be entertained?"

He asked.

"I'm sure this is a sad and pathetic excuse to try to extract information from me that I already

told you I don't have. But if you want to waste your breath and time, go right ahead. It

shouldn't be much longer before my lawyer shows up... so I got time to waste." I said as I sat

back in my chair and made myself comfortable.

"Well like I said when I first met you, I knew there was something about you and once your

prints came back I was able to pull up a copy of your birth certificate.... and guess who just so

happens to be the son of one of the most notorious drug dealers that our city has ever had...

that is of course before he died in that fire back in 96. Now you may have been a little too

Young to remember but your father damn near ran this city, there was not a single drug sell

Made without his authorization... he was like God to the drug game. Anyways, the guy thought

he was untouchable. Local police couldn't keep up with him and the FEDS didn't have the balls

to go after him... no paper trails and no fingerprints, and you could forget about any Confidential

Informants cause the last guy that agreed to testify against him ... his family found bits and

pieces of him scattered all over thirteen different states. They still haven't found the head

though... Biggs was very smart and calculated, he never left a "T" uncrossed or an "I"

Undotted... but his right-hand man Richard... you know the other victim in this case otherwise

known as Duce, he was a lot less strategic...

"Duce man, what the hell did I tell you about carrying a gat in my car?" I asked

frustrated as I continued driving.

"Aye Biggs man I know you say don't have them in ya car B, but you can't be out here dangling

In these streets with no heat on you," Duce tried to argue, yet his argument wasn't relevant in

comparison to the rules I go by.

"You need a muthafucking gun with you everywhere you go because you haven't earned the

same respect that I have in this game," I yelled slamming the palm of my hand against the

dashboard before going on. "How many times do I fucking have to say that gun's equal prints,

Prints equals tangible evidence, and evidence equals what?" I asked fiercely.

"Prison," Duce simply said, speaking in a soft tone. Without thinking I snatched the gun from his

hands and attempted to throw it out the window into a lake.

"Exactly and I'm not sure about you but...-" I stopped mid-sentence as I heard the sound of a

police cruiser's sirens going off. I look up in the rearview mirror and I see the flashing lights

behind me. As I slowly pulled over, I positioned the gun between my seat and the center

console.

"Look just be cool, it's probably just a routine traffic stop. Sit back, relax and let me do all the talking" I said as I stopped the car and turned off the engine. The young officer stepped out of

his cruiser and approached the car.

" License and registration" he said in a demanding tone.

" Is there an issue officer?" I asked, I could tell that the boy was a rookie by the way he became

all jittery when my voice elevated.

" I said license and registration sir!" The young officer demanded as he took a step back

Placing one hand on his hip where his gun sat and the other hand on his walkie.

" You must have no clue who I am huh?... here" I asked as I handed him my information. He

took the information and as he back peddled to his cruiser, I could hear him talking over his

walkie.

" Base this is officer Davis, be advised I'm out with a possible 13-04 in progress. Subject a

Frank P. Watson license plate F-ox, C-harle, K-ango 12...." He finished, but that was all I heard

before he stepped back into his cruiser.

" I can't, I can't go back to jail man" Duce kept saying out loud to himself rocking back and

forth.

" Man shut the fuck up and quit acting like a little bitch, you wouldn't even be sitting there

worried about going back had you just followed my muthafucking rules... When we going

somewhere and we need heat I have stupid little muthafuckas that's gone carry and shoot them

bitches, that's their job, that's what they are paid to do!!... and if they get caught up with the strap they already know to take the heat and their loyalty will be well compensated.... WE

DON'T TOUCH GUNS!!! Unless we puttin in our own work and even then we wear gloves, now

if you gone keep the mindset of a spot worker you'll get treated like one, but if you gone be my

right hand mans you need to carry yourself like a boss" I said as I watched the officer

approaching the car." Is everything good, officer?" I asked

" No, no it's not" He responded, flashing his light throughout the car as he continued to speak."

Is there a reason why neither of you were wearing your seatbelts when I stopped you?" He

asked.

"Actually, Sir, we unclipped them as soon as we stopped. We thought you were going to ask us

To step out of the car," Duce retarded ass blurted out before I had a chance to respond.

"Why would I ask you all to step out of a car that's not stolen, driver's license and insurance

Both came back clean and neither one of you seem to be under the influence of a controlled

substance?" Officer Davis asked.

"Listen... officer Davis my friend and I are running a little late for my sons fifth birthday party up

the street there at the Midnight Glow Bowl... so if we are all set here can we leave?" I asked

trying to divert officer Davis's attention from Duces dumb ass outburst, and just as officer Davis

was about to let us go his walkie went off.

"Base to officer Davis" the woman on the other end of the walkie called out...

"Base you are a go for officer Davis over" he said, holding his hand up to us as if to hold on.

"Officer Davis be advised that subject P. Watson is a suspected 3-11 and may be carrying on

his person approach with caution. Do you copy?" The voice called out.

"10-4 base." Davis responded over the walkie before turning his attention back to us. "You

know what fellas I think I am going to have to ask you two to step out of the vehicle one by one

and place your hands on your head." He demanded as he flaunted his pistol.

" I'm sure this is all just a complete misunderstanding officer, if you could just call your boss I'm

sure he could clear all of this up" I suggested.

" Sir, I'm not going to ask you again to step out of the car and put your hands up" officer Davis

said as he firmly gripped his pistol. It became clear that this rookie wasn't playing no games so I

just placed my right hand outside the window and opened the door, then slowly climbed out the

car and placed my hands on the back of my head.

"Passenger do not, I repeat DO NOT move until I tell you to!" Officer Davis yelled out.

"Am I under arrest or something, officer?" I asked as I turned and faced the hood of my car with

my hands now on the hood.

"No, not at this moment" He responded as he patted me down before continuing. "I am about

to conduct a simple search of the car, is there anything illegal in the car that I should know

about?" he asked as he began to cuff me. As soon as Duce heard the sound of the first cuff

clamp down he took off running faster than a fat bitch trying to catch a "buy one, get three free"
wing ding special.

"Hey!... STOP! STOP NOW!" Davis yelled as he quickly clamped down the other cuff then
hopped on his walkie. " Base this is officer Davis I need back up; I have a 3-3-1 in progress... I
have the driver of the vehicle apprehended, but the passenger fled the scene heading
eastbound on Lawton " He stated.

"Copy Davis, patrol 418 is enroute to your location. Any description on the second suspect on
foot?" The voice asked.

"Subject was a male, early to mid-twenties, clean cut wearing a black shirt with a race stripe
across his shoulders.... He was seated before he took off so I'm unsure of his height, but he
Was medium built..." Davis said as he sat me on the curb out of the way of traffic.

"10-4 Davis, I'm putting that description out now... e.t.a. on backup less than three minutes" the
feminine voice responded.

"Copy base" Officer Davis said over his walkie before turning his attention to me. " Who is
he? And why did he run!?" he asked, frustrated with the fact that he let one get away.

"I don't know who he is sir." I said.

"BULLSHIT... So, you mean to tell me that you're in the car with a muthafucka who you claim to
be on his way with you to your son's birthday party and you don't know who the fuck he is...?!"

He said displeased with my bullshit and as he put on a pair of black gloves that he pulled

from his back pocket he continued," you ain't got shit to say now huh?... Okay well I see now

that we have to do this the hard way, so you stay seated right there and don't move," he

finished. I watched as Officer Davis probed through the passenger side of the car as well as the

back seat before moving on to the driver side. As he went to open the door the backup police

cruiser pulls up.

"Davis what's going on here man?" the other officer asked as he got out of his cruiser

"Maxwell? hey man didn't think I would run into you again tonight, what you following me

now?" Officer Davis asked in a joking manner.

"Nah, I just happened to be in the area when I heard base call for backup with your cruiser

number and location. So, what we got?" Officer Maxwell asked as he looked around. He

couldn't see me sitting down on the curb because I was on the other side of the car.

" Well, I'm in the process of conducting a search of this vehicle, I have the driver over there"

Officer Davis said pointing in my direction as he went on." He's detained, the other suspect

which was the passenger that fled the area, and the driver claims not to know who the guy is"

He added. In the process of officer Davis talking, Officer Maxwell had made his way around the

car. Maxwell stood there with a mixture of shock and fear in his eyes.

"Davis.... Davis ah, do you have any idea who this man is?" Officer Maxwell asked as he

Moved a little closer to be sure his eyes weren't playing tricks on him.

"Yup, that's Frank P. Watson... the owner and occupant of this vehicle," Davis stated with

conviction.

"Nah man forget all of that... That is Biggs, one of the city's biggest drug lords. What the hell

were you thinking? Did you call this into the captain?" Maxwell asked sounding a bit

concerned.

" No, I didn't call it in to the captain. Why would I? And what I was thinking is that I took an

oath to serve, protect, and bring justice to the people. Drug dealer or not he'll be treated like

any other citizen I would have pulled over tonight. Now, are you here to back me up or stroke

his ego?" Davis questioned.

"Pop the trunk," Officer Maxwell told Davis as he shook his head full of regret. As Maxwell

looked through the trunk and Davis continued to check the driver side of the car the only thing

that kept playing in my head was the look on my son's face this morning. Maxwell finished his

search of the trunk and yelled out, "Clear!" He then walked over to me and told me to stand

up, and he had me lean forward against the hood of my car. "Davis man come on, you've

already searched the passenger side as well as the back seats, I myself checked the trunk and

there's nothing... Truthfully, I don't think we are going to find anything either. So why don't we just let this man go, and go our separate ways," Officer Maxwell said as he started to take the

Double locks off the cuffs. I looked inside the windshield and saw Officer Davis finally lift the

center console that separated the driver seat from the passenger seat and at that moment I

knew I was fucked.

"Ahhhhh... look at what we have here!"

So, Who Did It?

"But not to bore you with a long drawn-out story I was the rookie who found the gun that

Had your father's prints on it and put him away for two years. Luckily for him the gun was clean

So we couldn't connect him with any of the murders and shootings back then... I respected your

father, because he simply could have told us that the gun didn't belong to him it belonged to the

person that was with him that night," Detective Davis paused to take a sip of his coffee before

continuing, "Anyways while Biggs was locked up Duce took over the game, but once Biggs got

out the relationship between him and Duce was never the same. Word on the streets was that

Biggs was trying to step out of the game, you know turn his life around for the better. But Duce

wasn't feeling that so Duce put a bounty on his head. But since they knew who Biggs was and

what he could possibly do to you at any moment, no one dared to collect. So,

allegedly, Duce got fed up and decided to take care of Biggs himself. Then ironically Biggs

Turns up dead with a single shot to the head then engulfed by the flames in that fire that burned

Lucky's to the ground," he added.

"And your reason for telling me this, is what again? Like I was never told how my father died," I

fiercely stated. Detective Davis opened up one of the folders laying on the table and pulled out

three signed affidavits.

"See, I anticipated you saying something along those lines. Now these are sworn documents
or statements, if you will, from the three individuals that escaped the fire that night. And every
last one of them stated that they saw a young kid around the age of eight climbing out of a
window right before the building collapsed," he said.

"Annnnd I'm still trying to figure out your point," I uttered.

"My point is... you didn't hear about your father's death did you? No.... you were there. You
watched your father get murdered in front of you. But it wasn't until you got a little older that
you started to reconnect the dots and somehow you figured out that Duce in fact did murder
your father. AND you killed him!" Detective Davis suggested slamming the palms of his hands
on the table.

"That theory is not only idiotic but also pathetic. Even if anything you just said was
remotely true, why in the hell would I kill James.... my best friend! Someone who helped me to
become the man I am today!" I questioned. I tried to make the distress in my voice sound as
authentic as possible without making it seem like a sham. For a moment it looked as if he had
bought it, but then he started back up with his rigorous ranting and raving.

"See, the fact that you killed both of them isn't what's got me twisted. The tricky part is...
How did you take them both out? Both of their weapons were collected from the crime scene

And neither one of their weapons were discharged... So, how'd you do it huh?!" He yelled.

"I didn't do anything sir," I responded softly.

"Look here you sick son of a bitch either you killed them or you know who did! Either way you

played a key role in taking away the two most important men in your fiancé's life. Can you live

with that!?" The Detective asked. As soon as he finished with his statement, the door to my left

opened and in came my lawyer.

"Who the hell are you?!" Detective Davis asked.

"Your worst nightmare if the next words out of your mouth to my client aren't, "Sir, you're free to

go. Now it is my understanding Detective that the victim, Marcell Bradley, has requested not

to press charges on my client, correct?" my lawyer asked, in a more of a statement-like

manner.

"That's right... but-"

"So, then my client isn't under arrest? And has no warrants holding him here, correct?" my

lawyer interrupted to ask.

"Correct," Detective Davis simply said.

"So, if I am not mistaken, by law my client is free to go...... Unless they changed some laws

today that I'm not aware of," my lawyer added.

"Yes, Mr. Watson is free to go," he responded as if his balls had just been crushed. I stood up

and my lawyer opened the door for me. Detective Davis walked us out to the elevator.

My lawyer and I got onto the elevator and before the door could close, I looked at Detective

Davis and smiled.

"Hey, good luck finding the person actually responsible for those murders," I said in a cocky

manner winking my eye at him as the elevator door shut.

"Here's your wallet, watch, and cell phone," my lawyer said handing me each item one by one

as he went on. "Your fiancé said to call her ASAP! And oh, here's your keys. Your car is

parked right out front, " he added as we stepped off the elevator.

"You know it's always good to have you on speed dial Keith. Hey, swing by the house tomorrow

sometime and I'll take care of you," I said.

" L.A. you know you take such good care of me. This one's on the house. Oh, and by

the way my wife told me to tell you she said hello and that she loves her new kitchen.

Speaking of wives, you better call your baby she was worried sick," Keith said.

"Alright then Keith man, tell the wife I said she's more than welcome and kiss the kids for me.

I'll holla at you later," I replied as I got into my car and powered on my phone. Once my phone

came on, I synced it to my car Bluetooth and called Monique.

"Hello!" I called out once the phone stopped ringing.

"Oh my god, are you okay? What happened?!" Monique questioned.

"I'm good. Baby, I'm good. Everything is okay. What about you? What's up with you? Keith told

Me that you wanted me to call ASAP, " I responded.

"I'm alright honey. I was just a little worried that's all," she calmly stated.

"Nah everything's alright baby. I am sorry though for what happened. I just lost my temper.

And baby, I want you to know that nothing physical happened between Jackie and I ever," I

explained.

"Shhhh... baby listen there's no need to explain anything. Jackie and I sat down and she told

me everything. We good," Monique responded.

"Good... You at home or at ya moms? You need me to come and get you?" I asked.

"Nope I'm not at home or my moms," she uttered, sounding very suspicious.

"So where are you then?" I respectfully asked.

"At your house, cooking you some dinner, since you didn't have a chance to eat much earlier.

And guess what I'm wearing?" she said in a soft seductive voice.

"What?" I asked almost effortlessly then there was a moment of silence before she spoke.

"N-O-T-H-I-N-G!" she answered in a softer tone.

"I guess it's a good thing I'm enroute then," I swiftly replied as I accelerated just a tad.

"Actually honey... I need you to make a detour."

"Why? Are we out of whip cream or something?" I asked.

"No silly, I ran into Janel outside the funeral home after all the confusion from when the fight

Went down and she looked devastated," Monique said pausing for a moment, so I intervened.

"Okaaaayy, which she should have been..." I said trying to figure out where she was going with

this.

"She was telling me about how hard it's been on her and how she needs a little help with

packing up the rest of my brother's things so that Mama can go pick it up tomorrow. So, could you stop by and help her out?" Monique asked ever so graciously.

"Monique come on now baby you know I don't fuck with that young lady like that," I protested.

"I know, I know baby, but could you do it for me. Please?" She asked once more. The main

reason I'm so reluctant to go is because it's a 50/50 chance that this is a trap. Just a

fucked up way to get me over to her house.

"Ahhhhhhh...... Alright Monique only because of you," I said.

"Thank you honey, she said it shouldn't take that long so by the time you get done, dinner will

Be just finishing up and dessert will be on the table waiting for you," Monique replied in a

Mellow tone.

"It better be... I'll holla at you in a few, love you," I called out before ending the call.

I pulled up to what was once a shared house between James and Janel but now just

belongs to Janel. When I pulled into the driveway, I sat there for a moment or two just

Contemplating whether I should go through with this or not. On one hand she could be

genuinely grieving and actually need help, but on the other hand she could just be misleading.

I got out of the car and reluctantly knocked on the door and before I knew it the door went

flying open.

"L.A.... I'm glad you could make it," Janel expressed to me as she gave me the 'okay' to

come in.

"Yeah, well Monique told me you needed some help packing some stuff or something," I said

As I made my way into the house, the first thing I noticed was the fact that there was not a

Single packing box in sight.

"Yeah, she came and found me after that fight with you and Cell. Come sit. You want anything

to drink?" she asked.

"Nah, I'm good... I'm just trying to help you out with what you need help with and get back

home," I quickly responded.

"You should really learn to relax more often instead of being so uptight," she said as she

walked into the kitchen and poured herself a glass of wine before continuing. "Truthfully L.A., all of James' belongings are already packed up," she said like it was nothing.

"So why am I here then!?" I asked, sounding a bit frustrated.

"Well, honestly, we have a little business to discuss," Janel said as she tipped the rim of her

glass to her lips.

"Business? What business!" I quickly inquired.

"It's been a while since our last encounter, and I figured you would probably be more

comfortable in more of a home setting," she finished as she placed her glass on the counter

And walked over to me. Janel wrapped her arms around my neck and went in for a kiss now

Even though I didn't want it. I can't deny the fact that her lips were warm and soft.

"I need a thousand dollars to take care of a few things, " she said as she walked me into the

living room.

"Well, I only got 750 on me," I responded.

"That will do, you'll just have to work that other 250 off," she explained as she pushed me

down onto the couch.

"Nah, I could actually go up the street to the bank and withdraw it from the bank," I protested

as I tried to get up, but Janel wasn't having it.

"Nope... I would rather have this," she said as she grabbed hold of my dick before continuing.

"As payment.... now just sit back and relax, you did a lot of the work last time so just let mama

take care of you," Janel insisted as she started unbuckling my belt while kissing all over my neck. Now because of our last encounter, I already know that fighting her off wasn't an option,

but the main difference this time is the fact that I possibly have the opportunity to get my hands

on her laptop, so instead of fighting it, I just went with the flow. Janel slowly and seductively

Took off my shirt then pants before getting on her hands and knees while on the couch. Janel

Slowly reached into my black, polo briefs and pulled my dick out rubbing it back and forth

across her warm soft lips. She reaches onto the coffee table in front of us and poured wine into

her mouth and held it there. She then leans back over to me wrapping her lips around the head

of my dick and I instantly feel the chill from the wine currently in her mouth. While looking up at

me she started sliding down my dick inch by inch until she couldn't take anymore. Then she

swallowed the wine. Then she started to give me head, while she was undressing herself. I'm

not sure if it's the liquor from earlier or what, but she's doing a damn good job. I guess giving

Head was a turn on for her cause I look over and see her playing with her pussy. At one point I

had to refrain from placing my hands on top of her head. After about another five minutes she

felt satisfied with how succulent my dick had become and with how extremely moist her pussy

was. "I see you've been eating a lot fruits," she said as she placed her hands on my shoulders

and climbed on top of me.

"How can you tell?" I asked.

"Ahhhh," she moaned, easing down on top of my dick before responding."Mmmm, cause

your precum tastes a little fruity," she said as she slowly rocked back and forth. She was

Already close to her first climax. I could tell by the way her thighs tightened up around my waist

and how she rocked. I figured I would speed up the process, so I wrapped my arms around her

Waist and slid my body down halfway off of the sofa before feeding her a few long deep strokes.

"Ah.... oh my god... just like that.... just like that," Janel basically screamed out. Once I felt her

trying to pull away and run, I sped up the strokes and threw them harder. From our last

encounter I figured out that she can't take dick while she's climaxing. It makes her weak, so

because I want her to tap out I do just that.

"Ooooo... Daddy stop, stop, stop, stop. I'm 'bout to cum! I'm 'bout to cum," she moans out as

She digs her nails into my shoulders and her teeth into my neck. Next thing I know her body

Goes limp and I can tell that she just climaxed cause I can feel her warm cum sliding down my

Dick and dripping to the floor. I stand up with her in my arms and her legs wrapped around me,

I place my hands on her hips and started ramming her back and forth against my body making

sure she was getting every inch of this dick. With her legs already wrapped around my waist

She grabs hold of my triceps and leans back in a 90-degree angle. As I'm continuously

Pounding the life out of her, I noticed her looking down watching as my dick appears then

Disappears inside of her (kinda like those orange push pops back in the day). After a few

moments of being drilled in that position, I feel her grip around my waist weaken, and I see her

mouth continuously dropping open every time she takes a peek at what's going on downstairs.

Those were two clear signs that she's about to blow. So, I pull her upper half up to me and laid

her on the edge of the couch spreading her legs out as far as possible as I continued to

excavate deep inside of her, while rubbing on her clit. Moments later I quickly found out that

she was a squirter, and as she continued to climax, her body began to quiver and weaken.

"Mmmhmm, I want you to cum inside my mouth," she insisted as we switched up the positions.

Solely for the sake of getting this transaction over with I bent her over the couch, and while

holding on to her arms I began drilling the shit out of her. Busting a nut this time didn't seem like

it was going to be that hard considering the fact that she's way wetter than what she was

Before. I'm not sure but maybe the "home setting" was a little more relaxing and I just ain't

know it. I watched as she was digging her nails into the couch and screaming into the pillow

with each stroke that I threw deeper and harder. As I felt myself getting to my tipping point my

strokes slowed up and without even realizing it I uttered.

"I'm 'bout to cum," Janel swiftly turned around and began topping me off. So, I placed one hand

on top of her head and the other below her chin, as I started drilling the shit out of her face.

Once I felt myself about to pop I lodged my dick deep inside her chest cavity while pinching

Together her nostrils, preventing any oxygen from coming in or out of her nasal passage. I

looked down at her and watched as her cheeks began to fill up and overflow with semen. After

about ten seconds I could tell she was struggling to breath, so I slowly pulled out and she

starts gasping for air.

" Damn!" She stated out of breath after licking around her lips and swallowing what was left of

My kids. "That .... was amazing," Janel added as she stood up.

"Am I free to go now?!" I asked.

"Yeah.... the bathroom is down the hall on the left if you care to clean up, unless you want to

join me in the bedroom. I have an on suite with a huge walk-in shower?" she asked as she

gathered her clothing.

"I guess I have to huh?" I stated with disappointment.

"Nah, L.A. that was a choice I was giving you." She replied.

"Oh.... well in that case, I'll freshen up in the other shower and I'll be on my way," I protested as

I grabbed my belongings.

"That's fine, there are fresh towels in the closet. And you can leave that money on the kitchen

counter on your way out," Janel said as she made her way to her room. I made my way to the bathroom off the hallway grabbed a towel and cleaned myself up, but once I heard her shower

cut on, I knew that this was my chance to get ahold of her laptop. I slowly opened up the door

and stepped into the hallway, I first looked in the dining room and found nothing. Then I looked

inside the two bedrooms adjacent from each other and again, nothing. "Where the hell is it" I said thinking out loud to myself, and then it dawned on me to check her

bedroom. I walked down the hall and saw that her door was already open and once I stepped

inside I noticed the laptop sitting on the nightstand beside her bed. It was one of those sweet

Yet bitter moments because on one hand I have the laptop in front of me and on the other

hand the French doorway leading to Janel's bathroom was directly across from the nightstand.

now since that meant at any given moment Janel could see my shadow on the floor through

the ceiling glass that bordered her walk-in shower, I decided to take a different approach. I

quietly dropped to the floor and crawled underneath the bed until I reached the legs of the

nightstand. Once in position I reached up and grabbed the laptop bringing it down to the floor. I

tried to login when I opened it but I couldn't guess what her password could be, so seeing as

though time was of the essence I flipped the laptop onto its side and I snatched out the hard

drive. After placing the laptop back onto the nightstand and pocketing the hard drive I quickly made my escape. I dropped the money on the counter as I dashed for the door. I got in my car

and pulled off. Once I was about a block away I grabbed my phone out of the center console

and noticed that I had seven missed calls. One from my wife to be and the other six from Jackie,

so I called Monique.

"Hello," I said once the phone stopped ringing.

"Hey you, are you all done?" she asked.

"Thankfully yes!... I'm on my way home right now," I said.

"Oh, stop being so mean honey, how was she feeling when you left?" Monique questioned.

"She felt better than what she did when you saw her today....... but anyways speaking of feeling

better, do you need me to pick up anything on my way home." I asked.

"No honey I'm good, I'm just waiting on my dose of sexy chocolate. Oh, hey Jackie called me,

she said she tried to call you," Monique stated.

"Yeah, I had seven missed calls and six were from her," I quickly replied.

"Yeah, well she was telling me about how Cell had came by the house and damn near kicked in

the door as he was making all types of threats. She said he was with his little homeboys and

shit so she just wanted me to tell you to be careful," she informed me.

"Baby you already know I'm good out here in these streets....but I'll be pulling up in a few

minutes my love," I stated.

"Good, the door is already unlocked. Just follow the chocolate little path I left," she suggested.

"I gotchu .... see you in a minute ... love you," I expressed as we hung up the phone. I was about a block away from the house when I heard my phone go off, but I was waiting until I

Pulled into the driveway to check it. As I pulled up to the house, I noticed that Monique didn't

park the Cadillac back in the garage, she just left it in the driveway. So instead of being an

asshole and blocking off the walkway I just parked the Jeep on the street in front of the house.

I sat in the car as I checked my phone, and it was a text message from Janel which read...

"Real cute stealing the hard drive out of my laptop. The funny part is you claim to be educated

yet you're not smart enough to realize I can access my email from ANYWHERE! It's

programmed into my email, not my laptop. Good try though.... Oh, and Ima need fifteen

Hundred dollars in about three days. Holla." What in the hell was I thinking, clearly, I wasn't if I

fucked up the church's money like that. I didn't even bother sending a text back. I felt so stupid.

I just took the hard drive out my pocket and tossed it in the backseat as I got out of the car. As

I closed the door, I looked up the street and noticed a car there that didn't necessarily match

the Luxurious look of the neighborhood. It was cruising slowly, as if the driver was looking for

an Address. After the beat-up car stopped about three houses down from me, I no longer paid

it any attention. But once I took my eyes off the car and started making my way around my car

The sound of screeching tires stopped me dead in my tracks. The old beat-up car came

darting my way and the next thing I heard was gunshots. My life started to flash before my eyes
as I smelled the scent of burned flesh and felt the pain of hot bullets piercing throughout my
body.

While I'm sitting in the living room, I hear the sound of a car door closing, so I rushed over to

The window to take a look. "Daddy's Home," I said out loud to myself. The next thing I knew I

heard tires screeching up the street. I noticed the bright headlights then I saw

L.A. stop dead in his tracks before sparks started flying out of the car at him. I watched as

L.A.'s body twisted 180 degrees onto the hood of his car before slowly falling to the ground. I

Quickly dashed over to the door in nothing but my bra, panties, and a robe and ran outside.

"Noooo , no, no, no, no...!" I screamed out as I kneeled down and cradled L.A.'s head in my

arms. "Help.... please someone HELP... call 9-1-1..." I added once I saw a few of the

neighbors coming out of their homes to see about the commotion.

"Mo....Monique." L.A. struggled to say as he coughed up blood.

"Yes, baby...... I'm here..." I responded.

"I.... I..... I love..."

"I know you do, baby.... I love you too. What I need you to do for me is to save your energy and

hang in there, you hear me!? I'm right here baby." I said cutting him off. Sitting here cradling

his head in my arms. I couldn't help but to wonder is this it for us. I mean there was so much

blood it was hard not to have thoughts like that running through my head. "Hey, hey, hey baby you hear that? Help is on its way okay; I just need you to keep your eyes on me and

picture how beautiful our wedding will be," I suggested as I looked around trying to spot the

ambulance, that seemed to sound so close. Just in the nick of time the big, bright truck pulled

Up. Three men hopped out, but only two had a stretcher.

"Miss, I'm going to need you to step back," the man from the truck with the beard demanded.

The man kneeled down assessing all of L.A.'s vitals.

"Excuse me! The victim that you're trying to help happens to be my husband. So, I won't be

Going anywhere Brent!" I protested as I glanced over at his chest to catch what his name

Badge read.

"I apologize Mrs..... What is your husband's name?" Brent asked.

"Frank.... Frank Watson," I quickly responded.

"Okay good...... Hey Mr. Watson... Mr. Watson, can you hear me? I need for you to blink

twice if you can hear me..." Brent said as the other medic applied pressure to his wounds. Brent

then turned his attention back to me." Mrs. Watson, how long has it been since the shooting?"

he asked.

"I'm not sure... eight maybe ten minutes ago," I answered.

"Hey Brent, he has multiple gunshot wounds and he's losing a lot of blood. We need to get

him to M.S.I. asap," The medic addressing his wounds blurted out.

"Alright let's get him loaded onto this stretcher and into the truck," Brent stated. Literally

seconds after those words left Brent's lips and they put him on the stretcher. L.A. then started

Shaking really bad.

"What's happening? What's wrong? What did you do?" I yelled.

"He's going into shock.... Mr. Watson? Hey, I'm right here with you buddy.... Strap his legs in,"

Brent told the other medic as they rolled him to the back of the truck. As they loaded him into

the truck, I quickly ran and locked the front door then ran back to the truck.

"I'm coming!" I stated as I stopped Brent from closing the door.

"Mrs. Watson, you don't want to change and just meet us down there?" Brent asked.

"What part of I'm coming, didn't register with you?" I stated.

"Well come on! We have to go now!" Brent responded as he reached for my hand helping

me into the truck. Once I was in, he closed the door and banged his hand on the top of the

Truck. Then we were off. I watched as Brent cut the clothes off of L.A. and began to apply

pressure to the multiple wounds. "Mrs. Watson, is he allergic to any medications that you know

of?" Brent asked as he pulled out a butterfly needle connected to an IV.

"No, nothing that I know of! What is that?" I questioned.

"Morphine to help with the pain. So that he doesn't go into shock again," he answered before

turning his attention to his walkie. "M.S.I. this is truck 287 over.."

"M.S.I. to 287, you're clear to go... What's your 87?" the voice responded.

"I have a twenty-eight-year-old African American male with multiple gunshot wounds to his

chest, abdomen, and legs. Subjects vital signs are weak and he has lost a lot of blood. E.T.A.

is less than five minutes and we're coming in hot so ima need I.C.T.
there when I pull up," Brent
demanded.
"Copy 287, I.C.T. will be waiting for your arrival at the south gate," the
voice on the walkie
replied. Brent checked L.A.'s vitals once again and shook his head.
"Hey Sal! I need you to move this goddamn truck!" he yelled out to the
medic driving. as he
placed an oxygen mask over L.A.'s mouth and nose.
"Wha-.... what's wrong!" I asked, almost demanding to know.
"Mrs. Watson, I need you to have a seat and just talk to your husband. I
need you to keep him
awake and here with us. His vitals are dropping lower, and any slight
delay could be the
difference between life and death for him! So just talk to him, keep him
awake and alert!"
Brent suggested. I sat down on the bench beside L.A. and took him by
the hand.
"Hey... Hey honey.... Hey baby look at me. I need you to keep your eyes
on me, okay?" I said
pausing as I ran my fingers through his dreads before continuing. "Hey,
re.... remember the
first time we met? I was 13 so you had to be like 14. I had the biggest
crush on you but I
never wanted to tell you cause I was so scared of rejection. Maybe if I
said something, it
wouldn't have taken us so long to see that we were perfect for each
other. When you proposed
to me, it was like so magical and to be honest I wasn't sure if I was ready
because of the
Lifestyle you were living. But you gave that all up for me baby and I love
you so much for that!

And if there's one thing I know. I know that you are strong and have the heart of a lion. So, you

Gone get through this, you hear me?" I asked. I felt L.A.'s grip weaken after I spoke. I saw his

eyes close... " Hey... Hey!... L.A. wake up!" I screamed as I slapped him across his face in a

poor attempt to get his attention! But he wouldn't wake up.

"Mrs. Watson, please stop." Brent commanded grabbing ahold to my arm before turning his

attention to his walkie. " 287 to base?" he added.

"Go for base 287," the voice on the other side of the walkie responded.

"Please advise I.C.T. that the subject is unconscious, so they may need a defibrillator," he said

as he continuously pricked the tip of L.A.'s fingers with a needle.

"287 is this your unit pulling in now?" the voice asked.

"Yes!" Brent quickly responded, and just like that a team of people came rushing out of the ER

entrance.

"You did good 287... We will take it from here," one of the doctors called out as they rapidly

pulled him from the truck and rushed him into the building. "We already have an X-ray room

prepped and ready, we need to get this young man in and out as quickly as possible. The

quicker we get him into the operating room the better chance we have at saving him," the

doctor added as he and his team rushed L.A. through the halls of the hospital. I was right along

side of him until we arrived at the X-ray room.

"Miss, I'm sorry but I'm going to have to ask you to wait in the lobby, you're not allowed past

This point," one of the nurses said while holding me back.

"But that's my husband!" I protested. I watched as they rolled L.A.'s body right past me, aside
from the blood he had a peaceful look on his face as if he knew I was with him.
"Ma'am I understand, but this is hospital policy," the nurse added as she waved for security to
come over.
"Don't touch me!!! Don't you fucking touch me!!" I demanded as the two men approached
before going on. "Just point me in the direction of the waiting room," I said. The men politely
complied with my order and I made my way down the hall into the "family and friends" waiting
area. "Lord, please allow Frank to come back to me. I'm not sure what I would do if I lost him."
I said to myself as I was pacing back and forth in the waiting room before finally taking a seat..
There was no one but me in the waiting room. I didn't have my phone on me and for the first
time in a long time I felt alone. It had been hours since I had seen or heard anything from
anybody about L.A.'s status and as time dragged on, I began to worry more and more.
"Monique..." a voice called out.
"Yes!" I said as I quickly stood to my feet before acknowledging who had spoken to me. Once I
turned around I saw who it was that I was responding to, "Detective Davis...? What are you
doing here?" I questioned.
"My team had gotten a call a few hours ago to be on standby for a possible homicide and when

I heard who the victim was, I came down here as quickly as possible. "Detective Davis
answered.
"Homicide!?" I quickly responded damn near dropping to my knees.
"Hey, listen Monique, that's just the term they used. From what I hear he came here in critical
condition and he's in surgery right now." He stated as he motioned for me to have a seat.
"Yeah... it's been a little over five hours now and I haven't heard anything from anyone. Not a
doctor, not a nurse, not even a damn officer to gather a statement from me!" I responded a little
frustrated with the unknown.
"Monique I'm sure that the doctors and nurses are doing everything in their power to make sure
Frank comes out on top of this. And I drove past the crime scene on my way over. The police
are out collecting as much evidence and as many statements as possible while securing the
area. Which means that you are next to be visited so that they can collect your statement and
come closer to catching who did this. "Detective Davis reassured me before posing a question
of his own, "Do you have any idea as to who may want to hurt L.A.?" he added.
"No Detective, L.A. is such a loveable and caring person. He quit the line of work he was in so
I don't see why anyone would want to hurt him, let alone try to kill him," I responded as a tear
rolled down my cheek.
"His line of work?" Detective Davis repeated before hitting me with a follow-up question. "What

line of work was he into?" he finished.

"He was a DJ at King of Diamonds," I quickly responded, lying right through my teeth. I couldn't

throw my soon to be husband under the bus by telling Detective Davis that L.A. use to move

work. For one, I don't want them possibly bringing up drug charges on him. Secondly, it was

none of his business how my baby was making his money. Shit now that I think about it, it's

been a while since he gave that lifestyle up so how has he been maintaining it?

"A DJ huh?" Detective Davis uttered as if he knew better not to believe that, but he didn't follow

up with another question about L.A.'s work so I guess he's just leaving it alone but then he

spoke. "Where is his mother?" he asked.

"I didn't have a chance to call her. I didn't want to risk leaving the waiting room and the doctor

or one of the nurses comes out looking for me, and I'm nowhere to be found," I explained.

"No cell phone?" he added into his line of questioning.

"Detective, does it look like I had time to grab anything?" I quickly answered pulling down the

collar of my robe to show my bra strap.

"I see.... Well here, use mine," he suggested as he pulled his cell phone from his upper left

jacket pocket and handed it to me. I grabbed the phone and started to dial L.A.'s mother's

number and just as I was about to press the dial/call an older man with a white lab coat on

stepped into the room.

"Family of Mr. Watson" the man called out.

"Yes! Yes, that would be me" I sprung up and shouted as I rushed over to the man.

"Mr. Watson's chart tells me that he has no siblings, and you look a little young to be his

mother... so if you don't mind me asking what your relationship with Mr. Watson is?" the man

asked, sounding like an asshole.

"Sir, I am his fiancé!" I stated.

"I'm sorry miss but if you're not listed as next to kin or immediate family, I can't disclose any

information about his status. For all I know you could be the one behind this," he quickly

responded. As I felt my hand start to gravitate from my hip up to the side of his face, I was

Pulled back by Detective Davis.

"Hey, how are you, doctor.... Ah...? Detective Davis said, posing his statement as a question.

"Maruchan.... Doctor Maruchan... And you are.?" Dr. Maruchan asked impulsively.

"I am homicide Detective Davis," he said as he presented the doctor with his I.D and badge

before going on. "Do you mind disclosing his status now?" he asked in a very cunning fashion.

"No, not at all officer," Dr. Maruchan said before turning his attention over to me. "And

what about her?" he asked, pointing in my direction.

"She's fine, she has just as much of a right as I have to hear what you're about to say," the

Detective made it clear. My heart stopped and I held my breath as I paid close attention to the

next words to come out of Dr. Maruchan's mouth.

"Unfortunately, Mr. Watson suffered five gunshot wounds. One to the chest about six

centimeters from tearing open his pulmonary artery, which is the artery that carries the blood

containing carbon dioxide from your heart to your lungs then out of your airway. Another shot

was to his abdomen just barely missing his large intestine. The other shot missed his tibia by

An inch or two. All of those shots went right through him. But the last two bullets were lodged

In the upper part of his femur," Dr. Maruchan explained.

"But is he okay?" I questioned.

"We were able to stabilize him and pull the bullets out without damaging any of his major

arteries.

"Good, do you mind if I ask him a few questions?" Detective Davis chimed in and asked.

"I'm afraid you won't be able to ask him anything for a while. During surgery, even though Mr.

Watson was heavily sedated; his body went into shock which caused him to slip into an inert

coma," the doctor answered.

"How long before I can speak with him?" Detective Davis followed up.

"I'm sorry Detective Davis, but there is no way of knowing for sure when he will wake from this.

It could be hours, days or worst-case scenario could be years. It just depends on how quick

his body bounces back from all the trauma that it's endured," Dr. Maruchan expressed to

Detective Davis and I.

"Is it possible that she could go and be by her husband's side?" Detective Davis asked. The doctor looked over at me for a moment before looking back over at Detective Davis.

"Are you vouching for her, and asking me to hold you accountable for the safety of my

patient.?" the Dr. asked.

"Yes, I am," Davis said, interrupting the elderly doctor.

"In that case, yes you can go and see your husband," he responded turning his attention to

me as he went on. "He's on his way upstairs to the ninth-floor suite G-86. We tried to give his

mother a call but that number was disconnected. So, if by chance you have her current number

could you please give it to one of my nurses so that we can inform Mrs. King." Dr. Maruchan

added.

"Dr. Maruchan if you don't mind, I would prefer to be the one to make that phone call," I

suggested.

"I completely understand," the doctor responded as he placed his hand on my shoulder before

going on. "That's fine with me. I am sorry that this had to happen to you all but I'm glad we were

able to help. It could have been worse had he got here five minutes later, it would have been

five minutes too late," he finished.

"Thank You doctor," I said as I extended out my arm to shake his hand before turning toward

the elevator.

"Hey!" Detective Davis yelled out, causing me to turn around. "I'll catch up with you later, right?"

he asked. Instead of responding I turned back around continuing forward throwing a thumb up in the air. I got onto the elevator and pressed number nine like Dr. Maruchan said and once the

elevator reached that floor, and those doors opened, it looked as if I had just walked into an

elegant hotel.

"Excuse me... could you direct me to suite G-86?" I asked one of the young ladies at the front

desk as I approached.

"Actually, you can follow me. I'm heading that way as well?" One of the nurses who was

approaching to turn in a chart called out. I followed the young lady as we dipped and turned

through a few different halls before finally reaching our destination. "Here you go," the polite

nurse said, pointing at the door to the left as she went on. "Next time honey you might just want

to come in through the regular entrance, the elevators over there are way closer to this room."

she added.

"Thank you so much!" I said to the nurse as she walked away. Before I could even open the

door I could hear the sounds of monitors beeping and the oxygen machine going, I opened the

door and even though I tried not to I just broke down. Seeing L.A. laid up in that hospital bed

with bandages, an oxygen tube down his throat and a feeding tube in his stomach made me

weak to my core. I walked over to the side of his bed and caressed his face. "I'm right here

baby." I whispered into his ear before kissing him on his forehead. Once I returned to my up right position, I noticed the phone on the other side of his bed. I slowly walked over to the

phone dreading the phone call that I am about to make. I'm not even sure if I know what to say

or how to say it.

"Um...... Hello? Who is this? And why are you calling me at this obscene time of the night?"

Mrs. King asked as she answered the phone.

"Ma, this is Monique." I answered.

"Hey Monique, what's wrong baby? Why are you calling so late? Is everything okay?" Mrs. King

questioned, sounding a lot more alert.

"No, Ma.... Everything is not alright..., L.A.'s been shot... " I sadly reported.

I have been up at this hospital faithfully everyday morning, noon, and night for the past two

weeks hoping and praying that God allows L.A. to open his eyes again. Flowers and get well

soon cards started to fill up the room as the days went past. And each day I went without

hearing his voice or having him hold me felt like I died a little inside. I didn't really realize how

much of a hold this boy truly has over me until all of this transpired. I had the time to sit and

Think about what I want and deserve out of life. Growing up I remember I never had good luck

With guys, they would always start off awesome but then they eventually show their true colors.

Since I was a sucker for love, I was the one continuously getting hurt. Ever since L.A. and I

were younger, I have always known him to be a nice guy. I always had a thing for him,

but I never said anything because he was my brother's friend. Even when my brother turned

Him on to selling drugs I didn't stop liking him I just didn't want to seem like a groupie like most

of the girls in our high school and neighborhood. All they saw was his money and nice looks,

but I saw something special in him. I always have and I always will. Though L.A. and I didn't

spend a lot of one on one time together as kids, he and my brother were inseparable so

through James I was able to get to know and understand L.A. better. Honestly, I told myself a long time ago that if the chance presented itself for L.A. and I to hook up and make something

happen between us, I wouldn't be afraid to take it. I'm looking at L.A. from his bedside just

thinking to myself like I'm glad I took that chance because he is truly my rock. When I'm down

he lifts me up. He motivates me. He makes me want to be a better me. He's everything I could

have ever asked for and need from a man. He challenges me to step out of my comfort zone.

He shows me that I am worth much more than I think that I am. I'm sitting here just gazing upon

L.A.'s peaceful looking face and I'm so caught up in my thoughts that I didn't notice Dr.

Maruchan come into the room.

"Good morning Monique, I'm surprised to see you up this early," he said as he updated some

information on L.A.'s bulletin board.

"Oh hey, good morning Dr. Maruchan didn't even see you come in. And yeah, I didn't get much

sleep last night," I responded before turning my attention to the board. "What's that Dr.

Maruchan?" I asked.

"Oh, this is just a note for second shift to turn off his oxygen every hour on the hour for three

minutes," Dr. Maruchan answered.

"But doesn't he need that machine to breathe?" I quickly asked with a hint of worry in my voice.

"Yes Monique, but if we can trick the brain into thinking that it's receiving oxygen all on its own

then Frank might just come out of this thing a little quicker," he responded.

"But won't that kill him!" I protested.

"No, the brain functions just fine up until that three minute mark then after that it begins to

Panic. Five minutes would cause him to have a mental deficiency and within seven minutes he

Would be brain dead. Believe me Monique we are doing everything in our power to pull him up

out of this. I just need you to trust that we know what we are doing," Dr. Maruchan stated.

"Dr. if you believe that this will help him come out of his coma, then I am all for it," I announced

before turning my attention back over to L.A. as I went on. "The Doc and one of the nurses on

second shift said something about his sugar being low when they tested his blood sugar

yesterday, what's that all about?" I asked. I watched as Dr. Maruchan walked down to the foot

of L.A.'s bed and grabbed the clipboard that hung from his bedside.

"Hmmmm.... did anyone on my third shift recheck his blood sugar levels?" he asked as he

placed the clipboard back down.

"No, not that I know of," I responded. Dr. Maruchan stepped over to the sink washed his

hands and once he dried them, he put on a pair of purple gloves.

"Well, I see no reason to wait on anyone when we can figure out this puzzle ourselves," he

announced as he pulled out a pricking needle from his lab coat pocket. As he goes on "Do you

always hold his hand when someone enters the room?" he jokingly asked.

"Nah, I'm usually holding his hand about 90 percent of the time that I'm awake. I know that he can hear me and if he can't, at least he can feel my presence here with him," I said as I

Watched Dr. Maruchan take L.A.'s other hand and rub his thumb down with an alcohol pad.

"That's cute," he said as he pulled out this device that they call a glucose monitor. Before going

on, "But you do know that when someone is in a coma they can't hear or feel anything right?"

he asked before pricking L.A.'s thumb. At first, I thought I was tripping, like maybe my mind is

playing tricks on me.

"Dr. Maruchan.... " I cautiously said.

"Yeah Monique, what is it?" he responded with his head looking down at the device waiting on

A reading.

"Am I seeing what I think I'm seeing?" I asked as my eyes began to water up.

"Did that just happen when I pricked him?" Dr. Maruchan countered as he made his way to the

side of L.A.'s bed where I sat looking astounded.

"Yes!" I answered.

"Are you sure you didn't.."

"No, Doctor, when you pricked his thumb, he gracefully clutched my hand. I didn't move. I didn't

do anything I was just holding his hand like I usually do then I felt his hand lightly grip mine," I

explained rudely cutting Dr. Maruchan off. Dr. Maruchan pulled out his flashlight shaped like a

pen and walked back over to the other side of L.A.'s bed. Once there one by one he lifted each

of L.A.'s eye lids and shinned the bright light into his eyes.

"His sclera and posterior chamber have reduced in size and it seems that they are returning
back to normal," he responded.
"So does that mean he's out of the coma?!" I eagerly asked.
"Not just yet it means that he's trying to pull through. I'm going to put in for an MRI scan to
be ran as soon as possible so I can track how his brain waves are functioning. And I am going
to have the nurses dial back 15CC on the morphine we were giving his body for the pain. If the
MRI scan comes back good then we will proceed with running manual nerve damage tests,"
Dr. Maruchan said as he documented everything that had just happened onto L.A.'s bulletin
board.
"And what will that do Dr.?" I questioned.
"Well, first and most importantly it will let us know if his body suffered any permanent nerve
damage and give us an idea of how long it may take for him to recover."

"Nah, what ya need to do is get up off ya ass and walk on over to the bathroom," I said

as I removed the blankets off of L.A.'s legs.

"Come on baby, you know I need some help," he reminded me.

"L.A. baby it's been two weeks since you've been out of ya coma, now you know I'm here with

you 'til the end but I will not baby you. Now I tell you what, if you can get up and walk to the

bathroom doorway all by yourself, then later on tonight when all the traffic in the hospital has

died down, we can bake some cookies," I whispered into his ear. His face lit up when he heard

that because he already knows what "baking cookies" is code for... sex. The past couple of

Days he needed a little motivation to get up and get moving, so I would offer head as an

incentive. Even though as hard as he tried, he couldn't get up to walk, so if the thought of him

sliding inside this wet, tight, and warm pussy don't get him to move, I'm not sure what will.

"Baking cookies tonight?" he asked.

"Yup, tonight... All you have to do is make it to the bathroom doorway. As a matter of fact, let

me give you a sneak peek at what you are working for," I replied as I walked into the restroom

leaving the door wide open. L.A. started to lean forward as I slowly unbuttoned the pink and

yellow V cut blouse I had on. Then I watched as his eyes widened and his mouth began to water when I removed my knee-high skirt. I don't even think he noticed that my bra and panties

matched. He swung his legs to the side of his bed and grabbed his cane. "Come on Bigg Daddy... You can do it." I said in a subtle and seductive way as I began to

unlace my bra and once he stood up, I let the bra drop to the floor. "No puedo espera para

arsete El amor papi.." I added.

"Mmm... I'm not sure what you just said mamasita but I like it," L.A. called out as he shuffled his

feet towards me.

"I just said that I can't wait to make love to you papi," I quickly responded as I slowly inched

down my panties. I pulled them down just enough to see the lips of my juicy pussy, then I ran

my tongue across both my middle and ring finger before rubbing them up and down the lips of

my pussy. I can clearly see his dick bulging through that gauzy hospital gown, and the closer

He gets the wetter I get. It's been almost a month since we've last baked cookies and I'm giving

serious thought to just letting him claim his prize right here and now. L.A. got about less than

five feet away from the door when I heard someone bust through the door.

"Oh, you thought I wouldn't finish what I started?" a man with a deep voice called out. I couldn't

see who the man was because of how the hospital room was set up, but I could see the silver

pistol he was holding through the reflection in the window overlooking the city.

"Listen man we ain't gotta do this, what's done is done and we can just leave it like that," I

Heard L.A. say, and the whole time I'm in the bathroom looking for some type of weapon and

came up with nothing.

"What the fuck do you mean we can just leave it at that... Nah you looked me in my eyes as I

pulled that trigger so I know you saw my face," the man said.

"Look, I didn't see your face. Don't you think if I did you would be sitting in a jail cell right now?"

L.A. questioned.

"Either way I can't risk my freedom, for your life," I heard the man say before cocking the pistol.

Once I heard the sound of that pistol cocking back, Seeing the barrel of the gun peeking

beyond the doorway of the restroom made me spring into action. I ran out of the restroom with

nothing but my panties on and was able to grab the barrel of the gun with one hand while I was

swinging at the masked man with the other. He and I tussled around for a few seconds before

the masked man backhanded the shit out of me. Once I released my grip on the gun, he

rammed the butt of the pistol against the side of my head and I fell to the floor. By this time

L.A.'s legs had already given out so when I fell to the floor I just crawled over to his side. "You

stupid little bitch!" he yelled out, grabbing me by my hair and pulling me to my feet.

"Hey.... come on now man she has nothing to do with this just let her go, and deal with me," I

suggested.

"This a nice piece of ass you got here L.A.," the man said as he smelled my hair.

"You sorry son of a bitch don't you dare hurt her!" L.A. demanded. The masked gunman let out

a loud chuckle as he walked me over to the foot of the hospital bed.

"And what exactly are you going to do L.A.? Huh?... you can't even stand up let alone protect

this little hot thang. I'll tell you what..." he said as he forced me to bend over the foot of the bed

before going on. "You're going to be the one to determine how far this has to go. All you have

To do is stand up and I'll stop," he said.

"Stop what!?" L.A. asked. The masked gunman didn't bother answering L.A.'s question he just

placed the pistol to the back of my head and told me not to move before ripping my panties off.

Once I heard the sound of his belt buckle loosen I had an idea of what was next to come, tears

began to roll down my face as I watched L.A. continuously try to stand up but kept falling.

"Come on L.A. get up!" the masked man said. I listened as the man continued to mock and

laugh at L.A., then I felt him slowly run his dick against the lips of my pussy as I watched the

frustration on L.A.'s face grow. "Damn she's nice and tight," the man added as he slid himself

inside of me, the feeling was repulsive.

"You son of a bitch I am going to kill you!" L.A. yelled out as tears ran down his cheeks while

his arms trembled as he tried to get to his feet. The masked man's strokes didn't ease up in fact the more I resisted the harder and more painful they became. And in that moment, those three

minutes felt like a lifetime.

"I love you" I lipped to L.A. and literally seconds after I said that L.A. mustered up every inch of

strength that he had and stood up strong.

"Get off of her you bastard!" L.A. demanded as he charged at the gun man.

"How cute," I heard the man say before I heard a loud bang and the smell of smoke filled the

air, then I watched as L.A.'s body laid lifeless on the floor.

"Noooo!" I screamed out before hearing another loud bang then feeling my body grow

cold...Then I woke up... I opened my eyes and saw someone standing over L.A. with their back

to me. It was pretty easy to figure out who the person could be simply by the body type.

"Janel...?" I called out as I stood up.

"Oh, hey sleepy head .... Good to see you up," Janel responded as she turned around. I looked

down at my watch.

"How long have you been here?" I asked.

"Maybe about ten minutes, I would have woken you up, but you seemed to be sleeping so

peacefully when I came in, plus I figured you could use the extra rest," she said as she sat

down in the chair that I usually sit in next to L.A. sipping on her coffee.

"Did he get fed yet?" I asked as I looked through my suitcase for fresh clothing.

"Yeah, they marked it over there," she said as she pointed at the bulletin board before going

on.

"When I came in, they were finishing up. Is he doing any better?" Janel asked.

"Yeah, he's actually doing much better" I answered as I made my way to the restroom to
brush my teeth.

"That's good to hear...., but girl how are you holding up? I mean this all has to be stressful. First
you had to bury your father and brother and now the most important man in your life is laid up
in the hospital in a coma," Janel questioned.

"I'm holding up okay, I guess. Trust me it's not easy but he's the love of my life so we gone get
through this," I quickly responded before going back to brushing my teeth.

"You know Monique, I never thought to ask you but, how did you and L.A. meet?" Janel
curiously asked.

"Aw girl I've known L.A. for about seventeen years now," I stated before gargling.

(CREATE A BLANK PAGE FOR K.I.M. TO BE PUT IN LATER)

" Ma... I'll be outside if you need me," I called out as I closed the door behind me and

made my way outside. Once I get outside the first thing I noticed was the moving van parked

on the curb in the front of the building.

"Hey Mo Mo, it's about time ya mama let you out of the house," my friend Jhonay said as she

approached before going on. "Who's moving in?" she asked.

"I'm not sure Nay, I didn't see anyone on my way down. But girl guess what I heard?" I

responded.

"What you hear?" she questioned as we sat down on the steps in front of the building. Right as

I was getting ready to speak I heard the sound of the elevator doors opening up which made

Jhonay and I turn our attention to the doorway. Three men wearing mover's uniforms were the

first ones to come out of the building, and not too long after them this older lady came out.

"Hey Frank honey, you wanna come get your bike so that these nice gentlemen can leave?"

The lady yelled out as she pulled some cash from her purse to pay the men. A few moments

Past and we heard the sound of the elevator doors opening again and out came this little cutie.

"How y'all doing?" the boy said as he walked down the stairs then over to the moving truck.

"Girl stop staring," Jhonay said hitting me in my shoulder, but the thing was I couldn't stop. Not only was he a cutie, but he seemed nice. I watched as he grabbed his bike then he and his

mother walked back our way to go into the building.

"Hey ladies how y'all doing" His mother asked.

"Good!" Jhonay and I responded.

"You two ladies live here?" she followed up.

"No, she doesn't live here, I do though," I answered as I stood up.

"Well, I am Mrs. King, and this is my son, Frank as you can see we just moved in so it looks like

we will be seeing a lot of each other," Mrs. King said before turning her attention to her son.

"Hey baby, why don't I take this upstairs, and you guys get better acquainted with each other,"

she added as she wheeled the bike into the building. "Bye ladies," she finished. Frank seemed

A little nervous as he stood there with his hands in his pockets just looking around checking out

the area.

"So how old are you?" Jhonay questioned.

"9," he quickly responded.

"9? You don't look like you're 9...You look at least 11," Jhonay stated. Her observation wasn't

farfetched cause I thought he was around that age bracket as well. He stood about 4'11 with

long, beautiful hair, even though he had two braids going to the back I could tell he had that

good grade of hair by how his baby hairs on the side of his head curled up.

"Yeah, a lot of people say that, but I'm sorry, what's your name again?" he asked.

"Well, I'm Jhonay and this is my BFF Monique, but we call her Mo Mo," Jhonay blurted out. I watched as they shook each other's hands then he turned his attention to me extending his

Hand out. When our eyes locked, I noticed that he had a beautiful set of hazel brown eyes. As

I shook his hand I couldn't pinpoint it, but I knew that it was something about him I liked.

"So Frank, where are you moving from?" I asked.

"Kimbowle Ave. over in Murray County," he answered.

"Murray County? where is that at?" I followed up.

"Mo Mo girl you know the place ya mama take us trick or treating every year?" Jhonay

asked.

"Yeah, what about it?" I countered.

"That's Murray County," Jhonay stated. My eyes darted back over to Frank.

"That's where all those huge pretty houses are at?" I questioned him.

"Yeah, I actually stayed on the same block as the guy who use to have a scary movie playing

On the door of his garage from a projector every Halloween. If you've ever seen that house,

Then you know exactly where I was at," Frank answered.

"So, Frank, what made y'all move from that to this?" Jhonay asked as she pointed towards our

building. I couldn't even be upset with Nay for asking because I was wondering the same thing.

What would make him and his mom downgrade from living like the Jetsons to living in the

closest thing to the projects.

"Family issues," Frank mildly stated before going on. "But, hey it was nice getting to meet you

both, but I should go. Gotta help my mother out with unpacking," he finished.

"Okay, well it was nice meeting you as well Frank," Jhonay said as Frank started to walk away.

He stopped dead in his tracks in front of the door then turned around.

"Hey, please you don't have to call me Frank. My friends call me L.A.," he protested.

"Oh... so you want to be my friend huh?" Jhonay asked as a quick moment of silence filled the

air.

"Yeah, I wouldn't mind being your friend," L.A. said responding to Jhonay's question, but

looking directly at me and with a wink and a smile. And then he was gone. Since school hadn't

started yet and L.A. was new to the area, I didn't run into him again until a week later. I had

gotten onto the elevator on my way downstairs heading to the local park, and when I pressed

the "L" button for the lobby as the door started to shut half of an arm slid through the crack

stopping the door from closing.

"Hey neighbor!" a voice called out as the door began to reopen.

"L.A. what's going on? I didn't know you lived on this floor" I stated as he got onto the

elevator with me.

"Yeah, I'm over in 814..." L.A. said

"Oh yeah? I'm in 816 right down the hall. I haven't seen you in like a week. Everything

okay?" I asked.

"Yeah, everything's good just settling in. I don't know anyone around here, so I just stay inside.

Where are you headed?" He added.

"Oh, down the street to the local park.... Wanna come?" I asked.

"Ummmm, ah... don't know," he responded. The elevator stopped and the doors opened, I
stepped off and grabbed his hand.
"Come on, it will be fun," I protested.
"Alright... I'll go..." L.A. responded, giving in to my batting eyes and pouting lips. We dashed out
of the door and down the street running alongside each other as if we were in a race. We made
our way up to the park and for hours we laughed, joked, and played around with each other
Until we both were ready to call it quits. It was so hot, so we stopped by the store and grabbed
some popsicles before starting home.
"So, why did you and your mom move here again?" I questioned as I looked over at L.A. and I
could see all the hurt and pain in his eyes.
"Monique, you seem like a cool person and all, but I just don't want to talk about it," he insisted.
"Okay I understand.... Well why do they call you L.A. then?" I asked.
"Truthfully, it was a name my father gave me when I was younger."
"What does it mean?" I curiously interrupted.
"It means Lyrical Angel.... Once my mom and dad realized that I had a gift for singing my dad
started to call me his little Lyrical Angel and it just stuck," he answered.
"Well, Mr. L.A. let me hear something," I suggested as we finally approached our building. He
motioned me to have a seat on the steps as he finished his popsicle. Once he finished, he
opened his mouth and started to sing Dance with My Father by Luther Vandross my eyes
began to water because of how good he sounded. He sung about half the song before I had to

ask him to stop.

"What.... you didn't like it?" L.A. asked.

"No, I liked it, I just didn't feel like crying... but your voice really does sound beautiful," I

answered.

"Thank you...thank you.... I try," he responded, sounding a little cocky.

"Who is this?" a voice from beyond the door of the building hidden by the shadows of the hall

called out.

"Oh Lord," I tried whispering to myself, but was clearly heard by L.A.

"What's the matter? Who is that?" L.A. curiously asked.

"I'm her brother shorty, who are you? And what are you doing with my sister?" he asked as

he stepped outside.

"Frank this is James, James this is Frank," I said pausing and creating an awkward moment of

silence before going on. "He and his mom just moved in upstairs in 814 last week. He don't

know anybody over here so I figured I would show him around the neighborhood, " I added.

"Nice to meet you," L.A. said extending his hand out for James to shake it but he didn't return

the sentiment. The two just stood there staring each other down like in one of those old western

movies where you were just waiting to see who would draw their gun first.

"Oh, okay so that's you with the hot mom down the hall from us. Okay so what was all the

singing about?" James asked. L.A. didn't seem bothered by my brother's aggressive tone and intimidating size over him.

"First off I'ma need you to not speak about my mother in that way around me again. Secondly your sister asked me to sing for her cause she didn't believe the name that I go by was true,"

L.A. stated, in a less aggressive manner. L.A. kinda stood up to my brother which on one hand

I found cute yet on the other hand I just knew my brother was going to try to hurt him and then

the weirdest thing happened.

"I respect the fact that you're not willing to let anybody just say anything about ya mama,"

James said as he extended his hand out to shake L.A.'s hand before continuing. "Hey Mo Mo,

get in the house mama wants you," he added.

"Alright well it was cool hanging out with you today, we should do it again sometime," I

suggested

"Yeah sure," L.A. responded as I walked into the building but over the next two weeks that

followed I didn't see L.A. Summer break had passed and the school semester was starting and

still no sign of L.A. After the third day of school and still no sign of L.A. I finally worked up the

courage to go and knock on 814. I knocked on the door and Mrs. King answered.

"Hey... Monique, right?" she asked.

"Yes Mrs. King, hey is L.A. home by any chance?" I countered. Mrs. King looked down at her

watch.

"Actually, sweetheart he should be on his way home from school, unless he stopped by the

library. You want me to tell him you stopped by once he gets in?" she offered.

"No, that's fine I'll just catch him on his way up. Thanks though," I responded as I walked off. I
stepped back inside my house and went to my room cause from my window I can see in both
directions down a few blocks so I can see him coming. I'm not sure why this boy has my
attention when we haven't even spent that much time together, but he does. I look out my
window down about three blocks and I see my brother coming up a side street then I look down
a little further and I see two guys standing directly in front of L.A. and it doesn't look like their
holding a friendly convo. Next thing I knew I saw James pull out a gun and I heard shots get
fired. The two guys that were standing in front of L.A. took off running and L.A. was laying there
on the ground. James ran over to his aid and helped him to his feet. Neither one of them were
hurt and I watched as they rushed over to the building. I ran over to my dresser which had a
mirror, to fix my hair as soon as I heard their voices come into the house. I heard the
boys muttering something as I stepped out of my room and into the living room but I couldn't
make it out.

"What happened?" I asked eagerly.

"I don't know what you're talking about Mo Mo," James answered denying any knowledge of
anything before posing a question of his own. "Is mama home?"

"No, she's not James, but don't treat me like I'm slow I was in my room and I saw you shooting at some guys. James, you know I'm not gonna tell mama, I just wanna know," I explained. Both

James and L.A. looked at each other for a moment.

"I was on my way home from school and these two guys tried to rob me. Your brother showed

up right in time and scared them off with a few warning shots," L.A. stated.

"Oh my God, are you okay?" I asked.

"He good Mo Mo damn," James yelled out before turning his attention to L.A. "Ah... you

want a soda or something?" James questioned.

"Yeah, a soda is cool," L.A. quickly responded. James grabbed them both a soda out of the

refrigerator.

"Aye Mo Mo, let mama know when she gets in that I have company," James said as he walked

to his room with L.A. following behind him.

Three Days Later

continued....

"Yeah, so long story short, I'm not sure what was said in that room that day but

we've been apart of each other's lives ever since. And that unspoken chemistry has grown

stronger over the years. But enough about me, how have you been holding up?" I asked as I

turned on the water for the shower.

"Well, it's been a little tough but I have been hanging in there," Janel responded.

"Yeah, James told me you two were very close," I stated.

"Yeah, that was my baby, it still fucks me up that he's gone. But not worse than knowing that

L.A. almost died because of me," Janel responded.

"Because of you... what do you mean?" I questioned her as I stepped in the doorway.

"If I hadn't told you to ask him to stop by the house to help me out, then maybe he wouldn't

have gotten shot and be in a coma right now," Janel explained.

"Nah.... girl don't beat yourself up about it, it's not your fault. Whoever did this was waiting for

him to come home. If anything, you may have saved my life cause had I followed my first mind

and went downtown to pick him up myself, I would have been in the car instead of the house

and more than likely we wouldn't be having this convo.," I calmly said.

"Yeah, I guess you're right... Are you about to jump in the shower?" Janel asked.

"Yeah, hey if a nurse or doctor comes in just let them know I'll be right out," I said as I pushed
the door shut and got in the shower. Thinking about everything that has happened, I couldn't
help to ask why me.

I hung from the ceiling in disbelief that one out of the two most important women in my life was now dead. Watching my mother getting her throat slit then fall to the floor as she bled out reminded me so much of how I watched my dad die.

"See L.A. it could have been you and me vs the world, all I wanted you to do was forgive me,"

Bossman stated as he wiped the blood from my mother's neck that was on the knife

onto my shirt.

"Forgive you!? You wanted me to forgive you?! You killed my father you son of a bitch, I'm

just supposed to let that go?!" I questioned with clear frustration.

"First off L.A. I didn't kill your dad. Duce did and I told you that," Bossman stated. That feeling

of hopelessness started to settle in as he circled around me as he went on. "And we clearly

came up with a plan to take care of Duce, which we did. So, I'm not sure how I became a

victim," he added.

"I think I can answer that," a voice from the doorway called out.

"Du-......Du-...... Duce? I thought you were dead," Bossman replied shook as if he had seen a

ghost.

"Life is funny like that isn't it," Duce said to Bossman before turning his attention to me. "Little

Frank, you got balls son! Big ones at that! Your father would have been proud of you, too bad he's no longer with us," he added as he walked into the room.

"That's because you killed him, you sorry sack of shit!" I yelled out before hawking up a mouth

full of saliva and spitting it into his face. Bossman struck me several times in the kidneys as

Duce pulled a rag from his pocket and slowly wiped the spit from the side of his face.

"That's enough James," Duce said calmly before turning his attention to me as he tightly

gripped my jawbone in the palm of his hand. "L.A. you know I have come to notice that you are

one ungrateful son of a bitch," he added.

"What is there to be grateful for from you huh? Killing my dad? Recruiting me into the streets?

Showing me how to move a bag? Showing me how to be a thug?!" I sarcastically asked. The next thing I knew I felt the power of Duce's open hand come across my face.

"I showed you how to be a muthafucking man and not a soft ass little mama's boy! I was the

kind of father figure you needed in your life," Duce responded.

"Seems to me you were more worried about being a father figure to me then to your own son," I

protested as I looked over at James. "Ain't that right!?" I added.

"Aye.... Duce, what the hell is he talking about?" James asked and Duce acted as if he didn't

hear a single word James had just said.

"Nah.... go ahead and tell 'em," I insisted.

"You shut your fucking mouth!" Duce quickly responded as he wrapped his hands around my

throat and squeezed.

"Tell me what Duce?!" James asked demanding a response as he snatched Duce's hands down from around my throat.

"Duce is your father," I muttered after gasping for air.

"Is that true?" James turned to Duce and asked but by the look on Duce's face I could tell that he was extremely frustrated.

"Yeah James.... it's true, but now you see why L.A. turned on you. He already knew that if he

killed me that you would find out you were my son, and it would cause problems between the

two of you. So, he took care of you while he could. Son, I wouldn't be surprised if that was the

plan the whole time," Duce said as he handed James a gun before going on. "Shoot him! Pull

the trigger and avenge your father's death," he added. James racked the pistol back and

pressed the cold barrel against my frontal lobe. Looking into his eyes, I could tell that he was

fighting with himself trying to decide what to do. All of a sudden that "killer" that he was claiming

to be moments ago flew right out the window. I could tell that the feeling of abandonment as a

child started to set in all over again.

"Pull the goddamn trigger James!" Duce yelled.

"I can't," James softly said as he lowered the pistol. Duce grabbed James by his hair with one

hand and with the other he took a knife and ran it from left to right across James' throat, blood

squirted everywhere including my face.

"He was always so weak," Duce said as James' lifeless body dropped to the floor. "Where

did I go wrong with you two?" he asked as he reached down and grabbed the gun from James'

stiff hands.

"You went wrong killing my father, who at one point was your best friend. All because he wanted a better life for his family and you wanted him to stay in the game. See you thought he was going to try and get back at you for that shit you pulled that got him locked up. You went wrong not killing me that night, and you damn sure went wrong thinking you could make a better life for me than my father could when you couldn't even be a man and take care of your own kids." I said laughing out loud mocking him.

"You find this shit funny huh?" Duce asked, aiming the pistol to my head. "Let's see how funny you find it when I leave you just barely alive enough to watch me kill everybody you've ever loved then kill you," he added.

"Well, the good thing is it won't be a long list for you since you've already murdered my father, your son killed my mother so the only one left other than my best friend is my fiancé Monique," I said, as I said her name his eyes widened in disbelief.

"Not..." he stuttered to say.

"Yeah, your daughter. See with you two gone, I'm the number one man in her life," I responded. Not even fifteen seconds after finishing that sentence I heard four gunshots then everything went black. I tried lifting my eyelids open, but they were so ponderous that they would only open about halfway. At first all the white and bright lights bothered me but then my eyes began to adjust. I could hear all of the machines and monitors beeping which quickly gave me a sense of relief knowing I had survived that drive by, but at what cost? I wasn't sure. The

first thing I noticed was the breathing tube in my mouth. I tried to remove it but quickly realized

that my mobility functions were not intact. I couldn't move my legs or my arms. Then I looked

down towards the foot of my bed and I saw the back of Monique's head just bobbing up and

down slowly on my dick. I can't feel anything, but I can tell she's enjoying herself by the way

she's handling my dick with care. She keeps going for about another ten minutes and ain't no

telling how long she was sucking my dick before I woke up. Yet not once has she looked up at

me or even turned her head a different way. The longer that I am awake I slowly start feeling a

tingling sensation in my fingertips, so I try to focus all of my energy on lifting up my right hand

and placing it on top of her head. I channeled all my energy and mustered up all of my strength,

and I was able to lift my hand up about three to four inches from the side of the bed. But I

couldn't keep them up that long so they just flopped back down to the side of me. The subtle

thump that the bed made from my hand was enough to get her attention. She slowly turned her

head towards me and I could have just died at that moment. "Janel," I thought to myself as I

watched her wipe her lips off then placed her index finger up to her lips as if she was telling me to be quiet. She took a wet wipe from her purse and cleaned the lipstick off of my limp dick, then pulled my gown back down and fixed the sheets before causing a scene.

"Oh my God! Monique come, come quick!" Janel shouted. Monique came rushing out of the

bathroom soaking wet with only a towel on, then soon after a nurse.

"What...? What...?!" Monique asked.

"Look," Janel said, pointing over at me.

"I'll go page Dr. Maruchan right away," the nurse said before rushing out of the room. Monique

just stood there looking at me in total shock and disbelief as if she had reconnected with a long

lost friend.

"Frank.... Oh my God!" Monique yelled out as she rushed over to my side and wrapped her

arms around me. I could barely feel her touch but seeing her and smelling her scent was just

fine. The nurses and doctors stepped in to take a look at me. And while they were doing that

Monique ran back into the bathroom and got dressed.

"Mr. Watson.... How are you doing? I am Dr. Maruchan. Can you please tell me your

birthday?" Dr. Maruchan asked as he carefully removed the breathing tube. In my head I said

my birthday crystal clear but my lips didn't move a bit, so the doctor went on. "Mr. Watson can

you at least tell me how you got here or what day it is?" he questioned. But I still couldn't offer

him any type of answer. "Okay Mr. Watson, we are going to do a little exercise. I want you to

blink once for YES and twice for NO, okay?" he finished.

-Blink-

"Okay great... Are you in the hospital right now?" he asked, starting a series of questions.

-Blink-

"Do you know you've been shot multiple times?"

-Blink"

"Do you remember the shooting?"

-Blink-

"Do you know how long you have been here?"

-Blink-Blink-

"It's been almost three weeks now; you were in a shock induced coma. Lastly Mr. Watson,

do you know who shot you?" he asked. By this time Monique had come back and was

standing by my side holding my hand. I looked up at her then back at the doctor before

answering.

-Blink——-Blink-. The doctor turned to one of the female nurses and gave her some instructions

then returned his attention to me.

"Alright Mr. Watson, we are going to transport you downstairs for both a M.R.I. and a C.A.T. scan. One is to make sure nothing is wrong with your voice box or your physical capabilities to speak and the other is to give me an update on your brain waves. Okay?" Dr. Maruchan stated.

-Blink-

"Okay well let me grab my phone," Monique quickly said.

"I'm sorry you can't come," Dr. Maruchan stated.

"But I'm...." Monique started to say before I gripped her hand a little tighter, then she looked

down at me.

-Blink-Blink-. She stepped and shook her head as if she understood everything I said with the

blink of an eye.

"It's alright Monique. I'll wait here with you," Janel said as she stood up and walked over to

Monique's side. As they rolled me out of the room, I looked over at Monique I saw Janel standing behind her licking her lips as if the taste of my dick was still present. Once we got off the elevator, we made a few turns down brightly lit halls and in no time, we were at our destination.

"Mr. Watson, you're going to be in there for a while depending on how well your results are. I

recommend that you relax, but don't fall asleep, okay?" Dr. Maruchan said as they placed me on this table that rolled right in the center of the large machine.

-Blink-. The Dr. and other staff walked out of the room then I heard Dr. Maruchan's voice over an intercom.

"Okay, we are about to get started. Once I press this button the C.A.T. scan will start, do not

get startled by the sound and try to remain as relaxed as possible," he said. Everything about

the room I was in was white and highly lit, all except for the black hole that the table was pulling

me in. As I laid there in that dark machine, I started thinking about my life and the choices I

have made, some good and others were just what was best. This drive by just reminded me of

how brutal this game can be, and even when you try to walk away for the best... you still

gotta watch your back. I will never be a victim to these streets again and if that means I gotta

put another muthafuckas' dick in the dirt to protect me and mine. Then that's what I'll do.

Laying here trying to remember every single detail started to tire me out and after a while I just nodded off. I ended up waking up for a brief moment in the middle of the night and I saw that

they had wheeled me back into my room, when I looked to my far left, I saw Monique leaning up against the big picture window looking up at the sky. It was a picture-perfect pose the way the

moonlight bounced off of her soft milk chocolate skin. I watched her for a moment or two before

nodding off again. I woke up the next morning to the sound of police codes and light chatter not

too far from my bedside.

"Mr. Watson, glad you're up," the cop said after noticing my eyes open up. "I'm officer Quill

and this is my partner Officer Boomar," he added.

"How can I help you?" I said shocking myself, my speech wasn't perfect, but it was

understandable.

"We are just here to ask you a few questions, hopefully your answers can help us get the

savage beast that shot you off the streets," Officer Boomar chimed in.

"Where is my wife?" I questioned as I looked around the room and noticed she wasn't in sight.

"She's fine Mr. Watson we just asked her to step outside the door while we conduct our line of

questioning," Officer Quill answered.

"Do you know anyone, or can you think of anyone that would want to cause harm to you?"

Boomar asked as he pulled out a small writing pad and pen. There was a slight delay when I

shook my head "no," to Officer Boomar's question which caused him to ask the question as if

my answer would be different. "Mr. Watson, are you sure you don't know anyone who would want to cause you harm? You know that we are here for you and your safety, so if you know

something you have to tell us," Boomar stated.

"Nah... I'm sure I don't know," I responded. Over the course of the next half hour the two

officers took turns asking me questions like, "What color was the gun? What kind of car was

being driven? Was it multiple shooters or just one?" After a few rounds of questioning they

finally realized that they were not going to get any info out of me, and that's when the whole vibe between the officers and I shifted to the point where I started to feel like a suspect.

"Do you know this man?" Officer Quill asked as he pulled a headshot photo from a black

envelope he was holding before going on. "His name is Marcell Bradley." I pretended to take a

good look at the picture.

"Nah..., nope I don't know who that is," I answered with certainty.

"Are you sure? Cause he seems to know you, but he says you go by L.A." Officer Quill

explained.

"Nah... I don't know who that man is, I grew up in the city so there's a lot of people that know

who I am," I responded.

"Cut the bullshit!" Officer Boomar said with high levels of frustration slamming his notepad

to the floor as he went on..."You mean to tell me you don't know the man who's married to your

best friend, the man who just hours before the shooting was thinking about pressing charges

against you after the brawl that you all had after the funeral. Do you really expect us to believe that?!" Boomar added while I took another look at the picture.

"Oh... you talkin' about Cell. I hardly recognized him in this picture," I said.

"Yeah, well if my jaw was broken in three different places and my eye socket had to be

reconstructed I don't think I would look the same either," Officer Quill said.

"I did that?" I asked trying to remember the fight but only bits and pieces kept coming to me.

"Yeah," Quill responded.

"Damn well I mean I know Cell and I got into it and all, but I know he's not cut from that type of

fabric. He didn't shoot me," I said.

"How do you know that he's not the shooter when you just told us that you didn't get a good

look at the shooter or the car," Officer Boomar stated.

"I know exactly what I said and in no way am I trying to recant or contradict my statement. I

just know for a fact Cell didn't shoot me. I'm sure it wasn't him," I protested.

"Okay Mr. Watson I believe we are done here," Officer Quill said as Officer Boomar picked up

his pen and writing pad before walking to the door. "If you can think of anything to add that

could help us catch the shooter, give me a call," Quill added as he sat his card on the table

beside me.

"Probably won't be doing that but good luck," I said.

"See it's guys like you that don't respect the law and think it's okay to take justice into your own

hands. Nine times out of ten they end up getting themselves killed and causing more grief to

their family. Don't end up being one of those stupid muthafuckas that we have to call the
coroner's bus for," Officer Boomar said and no sooner than when he and Officer Quill walked out of the room, in came Jackie, Monique, and my mother.
"Hey you, how are you feeling?" Jackie asked as she gave me a big hug. Both my mother and
Monique followed up with a hug and kiss before they all gathered around me and took a seat.
"I'm alright, ...how y'all doing?" I asked.
"Look Ma! He did get his voice back," Monique said to my mother. I looked over at my mom and her eyes began to water.
"Hey beautiful, what's wrong?" I questioned.
"I thought I lost you," she said in a soft tone as tears began to roll down her cheeks.
"Hey, hey, hey don't cry. I'm right here! A few battle wounds but I'll be fine Ma," I responded
trying to comfort her.
"Frank... I thought you said you was done with the streets," my mother said with a hint of anger
in her voice.
"Ma, look at me. I am done, I've been done. I'm not sure what this was all about or even if it was intended for me but I am going to find out," I said.
"No Frank, baby you need to just leave. Why don't you go down to Indiana like we talked about
honey and just leave all this mess behind, " my mother pleaded.
"Ma, I'm not going anywhere and I'm for damn sure not going to allow some niggas to think they can run me out of my city" I protested.
"L.A. I don't want to lose you and I'll be damned if I lose you like I lost your daddy to these
streets," she said.

"Ma listen you're not gonna lose me, okay? I got this, I'ma make sure this situation gets

resolved and everything will be fine, okay?" I assured her. My mother just shook her head as if

she knew everything would be okay, then in walked one of the nurses.

"Sorry to intrude Mr. Watson. I just came in to check on you, do you need anything?" she asked.

"Nah sweetheart, I'm fine" I answered.

"Alright, oh and Dr. Maruchan wanted me to let you know that you will start your physical

therapy first thing tomorrow," she added as she walked out of the room.

"Thanks!" I yelled out before turning my attention back to my mom." Hey honey, you and

Jackie mind giving Monique and I a moment alone?" I asked.

"Yeah, sure baby no problem. Come on Jackie," my mom said as she stood up and gave me a

hug and kiss.

"Sorry to kick you out like this Jackie, I really do appreciate you coming to see me," I said.

"Aw it ain't nothing. I was just stopping by to check on you anyways. I gotta get home and get

ready for work," Jackie said as she gave me a hug.

" Alright well be careful driving and give the kids a hug and kiss for me, will you?" I responded.

"I sure will. I'll check in with you later Monique," Jackie replied.

"Okay bye-bye," Monique quickly said.

"I love you son," my mom said as she walked out of the room.

"I love you too Ma," I called out before turning my attention to Monique.

"What's up baby?" Monique said as she stood up then climbed in bed beside me.

"We need to talk," I said in a very stern tone.

"About what baby?" She asked as she looked into my eyes. I sat there looking at her in silence
for a moment, then it was like a lightbulb went off in her head. "You know exactly who did this
don't you?" Monique asked.
"Yeah," I simply answered.
"Who?" she followed up.
"Baby all of the details are not important. I don't want you involved anyways. What I need you
to do is go to the house and look.... -"
"Do you see this?" Monique asked blatantly interrupting me as she held her engagement ring
up to my face. "When I made the choice to accept your proposal I also made the choice to ride
with you through whatever, whenever, and however. You don't get to pick and choose when to
involve me and when not to. When you placed this ring on my finger that meant I will always be
involved. And it ain't like I didn't know you had a past. Baby, I know what I signed up for. Now
who shot you?" Monique asked again.
"This kid that used to work for me when I first started out moving work" I said as Monique held
my hand.
(CREATE A K.I.M.)

"Aye L.A. man I ain't trying to tell you how to run ya shit but as ya mans you need to watch the

company you keep," Bossman said as we walked up the street making our way up to Pop's

liquor store.

"Bossman, I hear where ya coming from, but Trigga is not a bad kid. At least not since I put him

down," I quickly responded.

"Yeah, well it's still something about the kid that I don't like. I don't even know why you put him

down with ya crew and not ya mans," Bossman stated as we got closer to the store.

"Aye man don't start, we done already had this convo twice. You only sell enough to reup and you smoke the rest of it. I need niggas that's really trying to get this paper. Like I told you when you put me on I was only in this to make sure my mama stayed straight," I replied as we walked into the store.

"L.A.!" a voice called out.

"Pops what's going on? How ya holding up?!" I asked and out the corner of my eye I see

James trying to cover up his face.

"Oh, I'm good L.A. How's your mom?" Pops started to ask as he came from behind the

counter before he turned his attention to Bossman. "Hey you! No, no, no, no, no, ... you

out!" Pops shouted as he pointed at Bossman.

"Get the hell out of my face old man," Bossman yelled back.

"Yo, chill," I demanded staring down Bossman before turning my attention back to Pops. "Pops relax, what's up? talk to me man.... Why he gotta leave?" I questioned Pops.

"That old muthafucka crazy and senile, that's what's wrong with him!" Bossman blurted out. I
pulled out my 9mm and placed it right below Bossman's chin.
"If I ask you to chill one more time. We gone have an issue" I said to Bossman as he looked in
awe before concealing my weapon and turning my attention back to Pops. "As I was saying
Pops, what's the issue?" I finished.
"Him and his little fake ass thug ganstas continuously hang in front of my store selling weed
and God knows what else. And every day I am out there picking up little baggies and small
containers off the ground and out the grass. And at least once a day this stupid son of a bitch
sends one of his little flunkies in here just to grab a few items and never pay. I'm sick of it
L.A., I told him that the next time I see him or any of his little ganstas I'ma put a hole or two in
one of the little fuckers since threats of calling the police don't seem to keep them away. What
are you doing with these clowns anyways?" Pops asked. I looked over at Bossmman who was still in awe, which was understandable seeing how today was the first time I had ever upped a mag on him. But at the same time, he was out of pocket.
"Listen Pops you have every right to be upset I'm not saying that you shouldn't be, but James
is a very good friend of mine and you have my word that him nor his crew will be slanging in
front of your store or stealing from you. Ain't that right Bossman?" I questioned.
"Yeah," Bossman hesitantly responded.

"See how quick we came up with that solution? We good?" I followed up.

"Yeah, as soon as he gives me three hundred dollars for all of the things he and his little crew

didn't pay for," Pops insisted. Bossman smacked his lips and muttered under his breath a few

words as he pulled out his bundle of cash.

"You heard the man!" I said to Bossman before returning my focus on Pops. "Anything else

Pops?" I asked.

"Yeah… and for the next six months he is not allowed in my store unless he's with you," Pops

added as Bossman handed me the three hundred dollars.

"That sounds fair enough," I said as I handed Pops the money Bossman had given me. "Hey

Pops is ya nephew working today?" I added.

"Yeah, son he's in the back taking count of inventory. You want me to grab him?" Pops asked

as he started behind the counter.

"Nah Pops you don't have to unless you mind me going back there," I replied.

"L.A. now you know you're welcome son," Pops responded before looking over at Bossman. "But what you gone do with him?" Pops asked.

"I'm going to take him with me. Like you said, if he is with me, he's good," I said as

Bossman and I made our way to the back of the store.

"So, you just gone let that old bastard finesse me out of three hundred dollars like that?!"

Bossman asked with a hint of frustration in his voice.

"Dig this shit here for one you was wrong and that's not how you conduct business and secondly, you're lucky that's all he wanted," I said as we walked through the double doors leading to the stock room and bent a corner.

"L.A., Bossman. what's going on fellas?" A young man called out.

"Trigga what's going on with you baby?" I asked as we gave each other some love, Bossman

just stood there in silence giving Trigga a grim look. Trigga was a caramel complected cat with

braids that went straight to the back, he stood about 5'7 and maybe two hundred and ten

pounds. Other than his "shoot first ask questions later" moto I could never understand why

Bossman disliked the kid so much.

"I'm good. What's up with ya mans?" Trigga asked breaking the silence that had once filled

the room. The tension between the two of them was so thick you couldn't help but to notice it;

and because I know Trigga has a quick "happy finger" I'm usually the one left with the task of

being the voice of reason.

"He's good Trigga. It's good to see you helping ya uncle out around here," I said as he and I

stepped off to the side leaving Bossman posted at the entrance.

"Yeah, well I took your advice about turning dirty money into clean money. I figured if I worked

here with my family then no one can really question my source of income," Trigga responded.

"Speaking of income...you got that for me?" I questioned. Trigga had become one of my top

and quickest dealers that worked for me in just a matter of two months.

"Yeah, I got it," he replied as he pulled out nine bundles of money pre-rolled and rubber banded

up," It's all there" he added as he placed them into my hands.

"Trust me I know it is, he said. I been noticing the work you been putting in for me and I want

you to know that your loyalty and hard work is valued," I reassured him.

"Aw L.A. man you know it ain't nothing, I'm just trying to get to this paper," Trigga stated.

"I know, which is why I have a business proposition for you and if you choose to accept. It

definitely comes with a pay increase," I said.

"I'm listening," Trigga calmly replied.

"You usually get an ounce or two of dog food from me every two or three days and at two

thousand per ounce you making, What? About eight hundred off each one?" I asked.

"Yeah, about eight hundred, maybe a few hundred more depending on the traffic and clientele.

"Why what's up?" Trigga countered back with a question of his own.

"Listen today is Friday, I got five ounces that I need gone by Sunday night. You ain't gotta buy

the ounces off of me at wholesale. Just sell the product I give you exactly how I give it to you.

Bring me my money and I'll have thirty-five hundred waiting for you to collect," I explained.

"Five ounces? L.A. man that's a lot to move in two days," Trigga quickly responded.

"Well... I mean if you don't think you're up to it, I could just find someone else to do it. I just figured you were ready to make some real money," I replied. I watched as Trigga pondered on the question for a moment. I looked behind us and Bossman was still posted by the entrance with his face still all twisted up.

"Nah, I'm definitely ready to make some real money... I'm just trying to figure out if this is a onetime thing or what...Like what happens after this?" Trigga asked.

"In a way this is a onetime thing cause I need to see if you are ready for the big boy table. I

mean don't get me wrong you being mobile is cool and all, you bring in what a little under twenty-five hundred a week?" I questioned.

"Yeah, something like that, like I said it could be more depending on the traffic and what not,"

Trigga answered.

"That's pretty good money but I'm trying to have you posted up in a spot clocking a thousand

dollars a day, but I just ain't gone throw someone in my spot. Which is why I came to you with

this task.," I calmly said.

"I gotchu," Trigga said after giving careful thought to my proposal.

"Are you sure?" I asked.

"Yeah, I can handle it... I have one condition though," He stated.

"Oh yeah.... and what's that?" I questioned.

"You and Bossman swing through to my place tonight, today's my sister birthday and I'm

throwing her a little party," Trigga said.

"I don't do big crowds," I responded.

"It's just a few of her friends but mostly family," he said trying to persuade me.

"Hey Bossman, what you think? You trying to go out tonight?" I turned and asked but

Bossman didn't offer much of a response he just shrugged his shoulders as if her really didn't

care.

"Alright Trigga we will be there, but I'm telling you now if I ain't feeling it... I'ma bounce," I

added.

"Don't trip L.A.... y'all gone come, have a good time maybe have a few drinks and if I'm not mistaken I said it was going to be a few of my sister's friends there," Trigga said as he patted

me on my shoulder.

"Yeah, well we shall see about that," I quickly responded.

"That we will..., anyways you got those five ounces on you right now or something?" he asked.

"Come on nah Trigga, when have you ever known me to carry work on me.... nah in about an

hour stop by Dutch Girl's Bakery ask for JoJo the baker and tell him you're there to pick up a

preorder of Boston Cream donuts. Once the package is in your possession shoot me a text

letting me know everything is green," I stated as we turned and made our way back towards

Bossman.

"That's cool I get off work in about thirty minutes anyways, so I'll be right on time to pick that

up. I won't disappoint you," Trigga said as we shook hands.

"I'm sure you won't. Hey what time did you say the party was starting?" I asked as Bossman,

Trigga, and I all walked up to the front of the store.

"About six.... six-thirtyish.... so, like four hours from now," Trigga answered.

"Well, I'm letting you know now I might be a little late I got a few pickups to make, but we'll be

there," I reassured him.

"Yup... I'll holla at you later," Trigga responded. Bossman and I walked out of the store and

made our way back down the street where my car was parked.

"So now we partying with this nigga?" Bossman asked.

"Chill man it's just a little birthday party for Heavenly, we gone go have a few drinks and try to enjoy ourselves. Plus, we could use a night out. I don't know about you but moving eight to ten

keys a week can be a little stressful sometimes," I answered as we got into my car.

"Whatever man, if we going out tonight I need to hit the mall," Bossman said.

"Good... cause I was thinking the same thing," I replied back in a joking manner. I pulled out

my phone and texted all five of my employees not including Trigga "23.25.1" which is code for "

where you at". They know once they see that code come across their screen they are to send

me the address of where they are at and stay posted until I come.

"Ha, ha, really funny... Anyways, where we stopping at first?" Bossman asked and as soon as

he finished talking, my phone started blowing up.

"That's weird," I said.

"Weird, what's weird? What's up?" Bossman questioned.

"They all just sent me the same address to that little mini plaza over on Beach Daily. "I

answered.

"What's all over there?" he asked.

"I'm not sure, but we about to find out," I quickly responded. I wasn't sure what to expect cause

all of the years I have been in the game never once had all of my workers posted at the

same spot for a pickup. Bossman and I pulled up in the parking lot and there's this massive ass

crowd of people lined up in front of Mr. Allen's.

"Oh shit.... I forgot that the new 13's drop today. Man damn, see L.A. fucking around with you," Bossman said. I finally found us a parking spot about three buildings down from Mr.

Allen's, Bossman and I got out and made our way down. I look around and I can't see any of my workers in sight. So, Bossman and I walked right up to the front of the line.

"L.A. what's going on baby!" The armed security guard blocking the entrance called out.

"Lance, what's going on with you? Aye look I don't mean to cause no problems, but I need to

get inside," I said as I tried handing him five hundred on the low.

"Nah L.A. man put ya money up. Yo boys already told me to keep my eyes peeled for you.

They inside waiting for you," Lance said as he stepped to the side allowing Bossman and I to

pass. When Bossman and I walked into the store, I was surprised to see not one there but all my boys.

"Jay-Money, Tae, Chucky, J.T., Bo... what's up fellas?" I said as I walked in.

"Sup Boss," they seemed to collectively say.

"What's up with the group drop off? Does anybody care to explain that to me? Why is all of my

money in one spot!?" I asked with heavy frustration.

"Well boss, Jay-Money had just got this management promotion here at Mr. Allen's so I figured

instead of you driving all around the city, I told the guys to just meet me and Jay-Money here

with the cash and we'll just stop movement in and out until you got here," Chucky protested.

"You thought that would be a good idea huh?" I questioned as I stepped a little closer towards

him.

"I mean yeah, why not?" Chucky answered. I quickly grabbed my pistol and before I knew it he

was feeling that cold steel going right across the side of his damn head, then he fell to the

ground holding his head. I racked the pistol back and placed it against Chucky's temple as I

kneeled down.

"You don't get fucking paid to think! You're a worker, you get paid to work. I would rather have

my work and my money scattered all over the city than to have it sitting in one spot. Cause I

don't even want a nigga to think I'm an easy lick to hit. Then to make matters even worse you

goddamn near a parking lot full of people outside those doors waiting for some new shoes," I

said.

"They can wait..." Chucky said as he sat on the ground holding his head.

"That's not the point, goddamnit! Do I have to spell it out for y'all??? With a massive crowd out there like that it draws unwanted attention to the area. Have you even looked outside since I texted you?" I asked.

"No.." Chucky said as he stood up.

"Well, I did, and I counted six patrol cars roaming the parking lot before I entered. This shit is

not rocket science you guys," I said as I glanced at everyone. I looked past J.T. and I noticed a

medium sized duffle bag," Is that my money?" I asked as I pointed in J.T.'s direction at the

bulky looking bag.

"Yeah, that's it," Tae said as he grabbed the bag and walked it over to me.

"Ah ... Jay-Money you think I can get a pair of those new 13's on the house?" Bossman asked.

His timing couldn't have been no worse, but I get it closed mouths don't get fed, plus there was

no way in hell I was going to wait around in that line with him for some shoes. Jay-Money looked over at me for confirmation and I just nodded my head.

"What size?" Jay-Money asked.

"A nine please sir, " Bossman answered sarcastically as Jay-Money started to walk off.

"You know what Money.... make it two pairs. I need a size eleven," I added.

"Coming right up," Jay-Money quickly responded. I turned my attention to the four other

workers who remained in the room. "So, I'm assuming you all are sticking to your regular

delivery amount?" I stated.

"Nah, L.A. it's some extra chicken in there from me, I'ma need three instead of two this week.

I'm anticipating a nice little rush," J.T. spoke out and said.

"Alright well I'll let the delivery boy know, when you call Pizza Hut just let them know you want a

"Triple Meat" half pineapple. The rest of you stick to the same code, Large pizza half pineapple

and pepperoni. My delivery boy Tony is telling me that you guys have been getting a little sloppy with how you're calling in. You call in and place your order, as long as you're using the same

address he'll make sure you get ya product. There's no need to be calling up there asking, "is

Tony delivering today?" cause I told all of you that the delivery days are Friday and Monday, if

you run out between those days then too bad order more next time," I said before Jay-Money

got back into the room. He came back which two boxes of shoes, handed them to us and
Bossman and I were off.
"Oh Jay-Money...." I called out.
"What's up?" he quickly responded.
"Congrats on the promotion," I added before walking out of the door.
"That was quicker than we anticipated," Bossman said as we walked to the car.
"Yeah, so I guess the next stop is.... the mall?" I replied as I tossed the duffle bag in the back
seat and got into the car.
"Hey shid.... since we got time, you feel like driving out to Great Lakes Mall?" Bossman asked
and even though I didn't feel like the lengthy drive, he was right we did have some time to kill.
"Sure... why not...." I said as I gave in.

"Well Jackie, I don't know what to tell you. That's the guy you wanted to be with so I

stepped to the side," I calmly said as I put on my shoes to get ready for this party that I'm

already late for.

"L.A. that's not fair man, if you wanted me, you could've had me but no... you didn't try," Jackie

protested.

"Oh, I tried Jackie, you just got caught up in your lie, but hold that thought someone's at my

door," I said as I walked to the front of the house after hearing the doorbell ring. I looked out of

the peep hole and opened the door. "Hey, I gotta go Bossman just pulled up and we gotta

leave," I added.

"Alright well can you at least call me when you get back in tonight?" Jackie asked.

"I'll think about it. I gotta go," I responded as I hung up the phone before turning my attention

to Bossman. "What's up guy?" I asked.

"Shit really...Who was that?" Bossman questioned.

"Jackie ass, calling complaining to me about her nigga," I answered as we walked into the

kitchen.

"Yeah, well nothing new there.... you ain't ready yet?" he asked me as he grabbed a beer from

the mini bar.

"Actually, I am ready. I just have to grab my watch and wallet," I answered as I walked off to

grab my belongings.

"Aye L.A. I thought you were wearing ya Polo fit tonight?" Bossman stated.

"Nah, I figured since I usually wear shit like that, I would switch it up with the Robin fit to go with

the 13's we got earlier," I responded as I walked back into the kitchen. "Come on let's roll" I

added.

"Hold on man let me finish this," Bossman holding the beer in the air.

"Come on, you can finish that in the car, let's bounce. We already late." I insisted.

"I didn't even want to go to this damn party in the first place," he mumbled as we walked out

the front door and over to my car.

"Hey, look inside that glove compartment you left that in here earlier. Maybe you should finish

that cause clearly you need to relax." I suggested. Bossman opened the glove compartment and out fell a little over half a blunt he was smoking on earlier today.

"Good looking, shit I thought I smoked it all. This is just what a nigga needed," Bossman said. I

watched as he lit the blunt and how the first hit seemed to instantly put him in a relaxed mood.

A little over twenty-five minutes past and we finally pull up to the house, and

there's a few people outside the house smoking and drinking, music banging, and the smell of

barbeque filled the air. As Bossman and I walked up to the front door, I noticed a few people

shooting up on the side of the house. They didn't look like fiends, so I just assumed they were

some kids just having some fun. Bossman and I proceeded to walk throughout the house making our way to the kitchen that led to the side door and backyard.

"L.A.! What's up, I was starting to think you weren't going to show," Trigga said as we

approached him at the grill.

"Nah, you should know by now that I'm a man of my word, plus I needed a night out," I

responded as we showed each other some love.

"I was told there would be liquor," Bossman bluntly stated.

"Ummmm yeah... right over there, help ya self," Trigga quickly responded. Once Bossman

walked away Trigga turned his attention to me. "L.A. what's up with Bossman, he got a

problem with me or something?" He asked.

"Nah, it ain't shit personal he don't like nobody. You just gotta understand that it ain't no such

thing as being friendly in this game. I don't trust a muthafucka as far as I can throw 'em.

Cause at the end of the day it's all about getting this money," I answered.

"I get that, but you and Bossman seem pretty close," Trigga said.

"Yeah, well I've known Bossman ten plus years, he was the one who put me in the game. And

over the years before he put me down, he earned my respect, loyalty, and trust. But enough

about all of that, what do we have here that smells good?" I asked.

"Well, I got some steaks, ribs, pork chops, some baked and grilled potatoes oh and some stuffed bell peppers, all the other sides and shit are in the house," Trigga responded as he flipped the meat on the grill.

"Not really a fan of stuffed bell peppers but everything else sounds great. Hey did you have any

trouble picking that package up?" I asked as I grabbed a rib tip off the plate next to the grill.

"Nah, everything went smooth. I was actually able to get rid of half an ounce on my way
home," Trigga answered.
"Good, good... you know Trigga I see a lot of myself in you, that hustle, that ambition and that
drive. Which is why I'm giving you this opportunity to move up the ladder," I said as I looked
around the yard.
"Yeah man like I said earlier L.A. I really do appreciate the opportunity man and I don't plan on
letting you down," he quickly responded.
"I'm sure you won't, but enough about business tonight, this is a party right? Where is the
birthday girl?" I asked.
"I'm not sure, shit she might be in the house," Trigga answered as he glanced around the yard
before going on. "If you're heading that way, why don't you take this in for me. You know that's
if you don't mind putting in a little work," Trigga said in a joking manner with a grin on his face.
"Ah, ha you got jokes huh. I'll take this tray in for you but just know I have no issue with
putting in my own work. But once you've put in the work I've put in, then you can enjoy the
luxury of growing an empire," I responded as I walked away with the tray of food into the
kitchen.
"L.A.." a soft voice called out as I sat the tray down on the stove and turned around.
"Heavenly...what's up girl," I responded.
"Oh my God, what are you doing here?" Heavenly asked as she rushed over to give me a warm hug.

"Well, you know your brother works for me now and he told me that he was throwing a party for
your birthday tonight. I figured it would be nice to see a friendly face, so I dropped by," I
explained.
"Wow.... come, come let's grab a drink we have to catch up," she responded as she guided me
over to the living room where the wet bar was set up. "So, what have you been up to?" she
asked.
"Nothing much really the same ol' same ol," I responded.
"I'm sorry, what did you say?" she asked as if the music was extremely loud, I mean it was loud
but I had an idea of where this could be going.
"I said it's kinda loud in here, is there anywhere a little quieter we could go to talk?" I countered.
"Yeah sure, follow me," Heavenly answered. We made our way through the dining room and
down a flight of steps. Heavenly led me all the way to the back of the house and into one of the
last rooms in the basement.
"Definitely quiet down here," I added as she slowly closed the door behind her.
"Yeah, well I figured since we had some catching up to do, you would want to do so somewhere a little more secluded cause if I remember correctly, you don't like being around a lot of people
that you don't know," she responded as we took a seat on the bed.
"You remembered that much about me?" I asked.
"Yeah, there's actually a lot about you that I remember. Unlike you sir I just can't forget about a
person like I never knew them," Heavenly responded with a hint of sarcasm in her voice.

"Now I wouldn't say that's true," I stated as I reached into my pocket. "If that was the case

wouldn't I have forgotten that you really like earrings and bracelets," I added as I pulled out a

medium sized black box and handed it to her.

"Oh wow... KAY's? It's beautiful, what are these fourteen carats?" she asked as she removed

the items from the box.

"Nah, actually it's a twenty-four-carat white gold matching earring and necklace set, but I'm glad

you like it," I quickly responded.

"I do, I really do like it. L.A. you know you were always a great gift giver, that was one of the

many things you were good at," Heavenly stated as she sat the box on top of the nightstand

next to the bed.

"Oh yeah, well what else was I good at?" I asked.

"Well if I remember correctly, you were always a good kisser, but then again it's been a long time you might not be so good now," she answered as she lightly bit down on her fingernail.

"Well, I mean there's really only one way to find out if I fell off or not," I stated as I slowly leaned

in for a kiss, she met me the rest of the way and her soft gentle lips touched mine. After a

moment or two she pulled away and tried to gather her composer. "Now you were saying

something about me falling off," I added in a joking manner.

"Mmmhhmm Nope, that was pretty much how I remembered it, just slightly better," she replied

with her fingertips softly caressing her bottom lip.

"You know what I remember?" I asked

"No, what?" Heavenly softly responded.

"I remember you having some extraordinary head game, but I mean like you said it's been a
long time. You may have fallen off," I replied in a more suggestive tone.
"Oh yeah" she softly said as she laid her hand on my chest pushing me down to the bed,"
Well like you said, there's really only one way to find out," she added as she started to unbuckle
my belt and pull down my pants. After she takes off my shoes she climbed on top of the bed and helped me out of my shirt.
"So, I guess I'm the only one stripping tonight?" I said. She sat up on her knees in the bed and
slowly pulled the dress that she had on over her head and as she tossed that to the side I
helped her out of her bra. Heavenly then positioned herself where her ass is adjacent to my face and her head is working its way down to my dick. I watch as she tucks her lips in over her teeth
and gnawed at my dick through my boxers before finally reaching inside of my boxers and
pulling out my dick. She looks up at me as she slowly wraps her warm lips around the tip of my
dick and eases her way down further and further. I watched as she closed her eyes and started
going to work. I mean it was almost like she was continuously bobbing for apples and if that
wasn't a sight to see her reaching back between her legs playing with that pink, juicy pussy
definitely was. The sight was so captivating that I just couldn't help but to rub on it myself. The
moment I start rubbing on her clit and the lips of her pussy she started deep throating the shit
out of my dick.

"I'm assuming I haven't fallen off," Heavenly stated after finally pulling her lips away from my dick and slowly running her tongue across the head of my shit.

"Nah, just like I remember it," I said. As I stood up, she immediately turns around and assumes

the "Doggy Style" position reaching back spreading the lips of her pussy. I place my hand on the arch of her back as I slowly ease myself inside of her and surprisingly it was just as tight as I

remember it. Without me guiding her she slowly started to throw that ass back and forth on this

dick and I noticed her moans getting louder. Once I feel her cum sliding down my dick, I wrap my hands around her waist and started pounding through her walls as if I'm trying to tear down

some shit. I watched as Heavenly looked back placing her hand on my thighs trying to soften

the blow of each stroke, which is only feeding my ego and letting me know she can't handle me.

Once I pulled out, she quickly crawled away.

"Damn nigga!" she shouted out, all out of breath.

"What?" I asked with a grin on my face.

"You know I would like to be able to use this muthafucka again after tonight. You know I like it

rough but damn boy," she answered as she laid across the bed.

"Nah, ya nigga clearly haven't been doing you right," I said as I climbed in the bed. I laid across

the bed and she climbed on top of me and eased my dick inside of her. She just sat on my dick

slowly rocking back and forth. She never offered a response to my last statement she only

rolled her eyes and continued to ride me. I let her do her thang for a while then I reached up wrapping my hands around her neck and slightly applied pressured, as I follow her motion with

my strokes. I can see the redness start to show in her face from the lack of blood flow so I

release my grip and as soon as I do, that sends her into overdrive. She slowly spins around

with my dick still inside, and she arches her back to the point where all I see is her ass and my

dick inside her warm, wet pussy. She starts slowly rocking back and forth on my dick and it's

kinda mind blowing just watching her pussy muscles constrict around my dick. I finally feel

myself getting ready to cum so I push her forward onto her stomach, I climb on top of her and

begin drilling her soul.

"I'm bouta cum," Heavenly yelled out with a loud moan.

"Yeah well.... I am too! Where do you want it?" I asked.

"Mmmm all over my ass!" she screamed out as I continued throwing dick deep in her. After a

few more strokes she squirted all over me and right when she was about to tap out, I pulled out

and bust all over her ass. We both let out moans of satisfaction, but as I was cumming I looked up

and saw Trigga standing in the doorway.

(CREATE A BLANK PAGE FOR K.I.M. TO BE PUT IN LATER)

I'm Sure It Wasn't Him Continued....

"So, you telling me that some nigga named Trigga shot you because you slept with his sister

years ago!? That's not adding up to me L.A. If he felt that way then why didn't he shoot you

back then? Frank if you're cheating on me with this bitch man just let me know, don't try and treat me like I'm stupid telling me this shit between y'all happened years ago," Monique fiercely

stated as tears began to roll down her eyes.

"Are you done?" I asked as I adjusted my upper bed level reaching out for her hand.

"Say what you gonna say L.A." she replied as she folded her arms.

"First off baby ain't nobody cheating on you with nobody and what happened between Heavenly and I did happen years ago but that's not the reason Trigga shot me," I said grabbing

Monique's arm pulling her over to me.

"So why did he shoot you Frank?" She asked.

"You remember that shoot out that ya brother got into?" I asked.

"Yeah, but what does that have to do with anything?" she countered as she sat down on the

bed next to me.

"Two of the guys that Bossman ended up killing were related to Trigga. The youngest one Lil

Vel was his little brother and Rockett was his little cousin," I explained.

"Oh my God," she said in a light tone as her hands came together forming prayer hands over

her nose and mouth.

"Yeah, and I'm so stupid because when I blew down on him and his family once I found out, he told me that everything was good. So basically, he was rocking me to sleep cause now

Bossman's dead and I done got lit up," I responded.

"Well, he should be dead by now, right? I mean don't y'all got like a street rule for biting the

hand that feeds you?" Monique questioned.

"Yeah, we got something like that," I answered.

"Well good, there's nothing to worry about. You make a few calls and he's gone right?"

Monique asked.

"And it would be as simple as that baby, if I didn't give up my rank my position of power, and my shot caller status for you," I answered. The room grew silent and the look in her eyes was one

as if she felt like this in some way was all her fault. I looked at the table near the door and I saw

a medium sized teddy bear holding a vase of flowers," Hey baby. Who is that from?" I asked

as I pointed in the area of the door.

"Ummmm some guy named J.T. dropped it off. Him and two other guys stopped by here a few

times last week. When he dropped the bear off, he told me to have you call him when you wake

up," she answered.

"Bring me that bear," I demanded. I could tell there was something off about the bear, it just

looked odd.

"It has a little weight to it baby, I guess it's one of those talking and dancing bears," Monique

said as she handed me the bear. I turned the bear around and noticed a slit down its back. I

reached inside the bear and I felt a handle of some sort, so I pulled it out," Oh my god..."

Monique softly added.

"Get me my phone," I demanded as I tossed the now empty bear to the floor.

"Your vitals are getting back to normal, and I'm told that your physical therapy is going good.
At this rate we should be able to discharge you in a few days," Dr. Maruchan explained.
"That's good news Doc. So, what about these knee pains?" I asked.
"I'll have the nurse get you a script for the additional pain meds but other than that you are as
healthy as a horse. It may help too if you and the Mrs. hold off on the hanky panky until you
fully recover," the doctor responded.
"I'm sorry Doc. I'm not sure what you're talking about," I replied.
"Oh nonsense, this one is a screamer. My staff tells me everything, but good day
Mr. Watson," Dr. Maruchan stated as he exited the room.
"I told you someone was listening," Monique said as she hit me across my chest.
"Girl, wasn't nobody listening. Maybe if you weren't in here screaming like someone was trying
to kill you then no one would have heard you last night," I replied.
"Oh well excuse me. I couldn't help myself asshole," she quickly responded before the knock
at the door.
"Come in," Monique and I announced. As the door opened, I reached for the pistol that I had
stashed under my pillow.
"What's up Boss?" J.T. happily yelled out.
"J.T., Tae, Jay-Money what's up fellas y'all a little early," I said before turning my attention to
Monique, "Hey baby you mind giving us a minute?" I asked.

"Sure baby," She simply answered as she gave me a kiss. " Hi boys, bye boys," She added

as she walked out of the door.

"That's a nice piece of ass you've got there boss," Jay-Money calmly said.

"Have some goddamn respect," J.T. said after smacking Jay-Money upside his head.

"Oh, that must be the one you walked away from this lifestyle for?" Tae questioned.

"Yeah, that's her," I answered.

"Well, yeah in that case I'm with Jay-Money that is a nice piece of ass then," Tae said as we all

shared a laugh.

"Damn L.A. man, I know this might not be the best time to tell you this but, man you look like

shit," J.T. stated.

"I feel like shit too man. But the Doc say I'm good and they should be discharging me in a few

Days, so all is well. Aye what's up with Chucky I thought he was coming as well?" I asked.

"Nah that hoe ass nigga decided to side with Trigga after he heard what went down," Jay-Money stated.

"Nah he ain't no hoe ass nigga, he just misplaced his loyalty," I responded.

"Nope, he still a hoe ass nigga," they all said simultaneously.

"So, speaking of this bitch made nigga Trigga, what you trying to do? Cause he around the hood spitting all types of venom on your name. Talking about how he had ya bitch ass on ya knees

begging for your life. That's why he only shot you up instead of killing you and shit," J.T. said.

"Yeah L.A. and once we found out what happened we was like we can't be a part of that type of fuckery so we dipped off and now we are all doing our own thang," Tae stated.

"Yeah, well, that nigga definitely got to get dealt with. But y'all already know I don't like shit done sloppy. I need to know where that nigga stay at. I wanna know where his mama stay at, if he

got kids, I wanna know what school or daycare they go to. EVERYTHING! Favorite bar, night

club, liquor store. Every bit of information that you can gather on this bitch, I want it," I

protested.

"We got you boss. Aye did you get that teddy bear I sent you?" Jay-Money asked with a

grin on his face.

"Yeah, I did. And I gotta hand it to you money that was pretty smart you stuffing a baby 40

inside the bear," I replied.

"Yeah, I figured you might need it just in case Trigga had enough balls to come up here,"

Jay-Money added.

"We all know he ain't cut like that. But how were you able to slide past security with that?" I

questioned.

"Oh, I just acted as if I had Down Syndrome they didn't check me at all," Jay-Money answered

as we all shared another laugh.

"L.A., you know man you ain't even gotta wait to get all that info just give me the word and we'll

go clip dog's cable tonight," J.T. eagerly stated.

"Nah J.T. that's not how we gonna do this. I want y'all to gather all of that information and wait for the green light code. Y'all remember what it is right?" I asked.

"Yeah," They collectively answered.

"Good, when y'all go back to the hood act normal, don't tell nobody we spoke. Don't even tell
them I'm out of my coma. If y'all run into Trigga or anybody in his click, play it smooth like there
was never any beef. I want y'all to keep him close, "I commanded.
"Why boss, if we gone do this nigga in why we playing that friend roll?" Tae questioned.
"Cause it's always good to keep ya friends close but your enemies closer. This ain't checkers
this is chess don't just suit up for battle, be prepared for war. Never let your right hand know
what your left hand is thinking.

"No stop it, I wanna watch The Real," Monique cried out in laughter as I continued to tickle her

in hopes that she would relinquish the remote.

"Nah woman, you've been watching ya little shows all day. I'm trying to catch The Walking

Dead," I responded and even though Monique is extremely ticklish she was determined not to let go of her grip.

"Knock... knock," yelled out a familiar voice.

"Come on in Dr. Maruchan," I insisted.

"Well, Mr. Watson I have good news for you and bad news for you, which would you like to hear first?" Dr. Maruchan asked, totally changing the aura of the room.

"The bad news," I answered as my heart began to race and Monique tightly gripped my hand.

"The bad news is unfortunately you're going to be leaving us.," he stated. Man did Monique

and I feel relieved.

"Well, what's the good news?" Monique inquired.

"Good news is, I have your discharge papers right here," Dr. Maruchan answered as he pulled

the pink papers from his clipboard.

"Damn Doc, you made me a little worried there," I responded as I sat up.

"Yeah, well it's rare that I get a patient like you with a loving support team that's just so easy to

work with so y'alls presence will be missed," Dr. Maruchan replied.

"Aw that's so sweet, you guys were awesome as well," Monique stated as she gave Dr.

Maruchan a hug.

"Now seeing as though it's late, it's totally up to you guys if you want to leave right now or wait
until tomorrow morning," Dr. Maruchan explained. Monique and I looked at each other for a
moment.

"It's up to you honey. What you wanna do?" Monique asked.

"Well Doc, seeing as though this beautiful young lady deserves a night out. I think we are
going to go ahead and leave now," I answered.

"Alrighty then I'll just send Nurse Cat up to get you all unplugged so we can send you on your
way," Dr. Maruchan said as he extended his hand to shake mine.

"Doc.... I'm not sure if I told you this or not but thank you!" I responded as I shook his hand.

"No need to thank me. I'm just doing my job," he replied.

"Hey, hey, hey family," a familiar voice called out from the doorway.

"Well, I'm going to leave you all to it," Dr. Maruchan said as he walked out of the room and in
walked the devil.

"Hey girl, it's crazy how your timing couldn't have been more perfect," Monique stated.

"Yeah, I know you said nine, but I figured I'll come up a few minutes early, but what's up? Hey
L.A." Janel said as she sat her purse down below the T.V.

"They just brought him his discharge papers, so we are about to pack up and go home, get
dressed and my king is taking his queen out to dinner. We just waiting on Nurse Cat to come
and oh, there she is," Monique explained as Nurse Cat started pulling out the IV's and what
not.

"Biiitch you know what's crazy, I wasn't going to tell you until I got here but I had booked us

reservations for that new French spot down here I was telling you about. Since they're

discharging him, why don't you and L.A. go," Janel suggested.

"Janel are you sure? You've been trying to get a reservation for that place for weeks now,"

Monique asked.

"Yeah girl, after everything that went down. You two deserve a romantic night out but the

reservations are at ten, so you won't have time to drive all the way home get him showered and

dressed then drive all the way back down here," Janel simply stated.

"You might be right, do you mind staying here packing our stuff while I run to the house, get

dressed, cause I showered less than an hour ago and I'ma grab him a suit? I won't be long,"

Monique asked.

"No!" I protested with a slightly projected voice before returning back to my inside voice, "Baby

why don't you stay, and she goes and gets the suit?" I asked.

"Because honey I still have to get dressed and I'm not sure what I want to wear. Plus, she don't

know what suit I wanna see you in and you know you keep all your watches and jewelry locked

up and she doesn't know the code," Monique answered.

"Then I'll go with you," I pleaded.

"L.A. the reservation is at ten, and it's five minutes to nine right now. Janel's right honey if I

take you with me we won't make it in time to the reservation. If I go now, you can shower here, the room will be packed up then once I get back all you have to do is get dressed and we

are out of here. Okay?" Monique questioned.

"Yeah okay," I sadly said as I slouched back in the bed.

"Alright... I'll be back," Monique said as she kissed me on the forehead before dashing out of

the door. Moments later I heard the sound of a latch clicking over and when I looked over at the

door I saw Janel walking over towards me with a grin on her face.

"I'm going to go ahead and hop in the shower now," I said as I sat up.

"What are you in a rush to do that for?" she asked as she pushed me back down and fully

mounted me before going on. "You know it's always been like a secret fantasy of mine to get

fucked in a hospital. And I mean ever since you made me feel like my head game

was so phenomenal that it pulled you right out of your coma," Janel said as she ran her index

finger up and down my neck.

"First off that's not what pulled me out of that coma. Secondly, why the fuck would you do some

shit like that knowing my fiancé was in the next room over!?" I questioned with high levels of

irritation in my voice.

"Because I hadn't had any in a while and my tonsils were starting to get a little lonely," Janel

said as she lifted up my hospital gown and started to slowly stroke my dick.

"Can you please stop," I asked.

"Awww you're so cute when you beg," she responded before stopping only to run her wet tongue across the palm of her hand then continued stroking.

"I said STOP!" I shouted as I sat up grabbing her hands. She snatched away from me then
slapped the shit out of me.
"Your little accident must have made you forget our arrangement. I get dick when I want it,
where I want, and how I want it. This dick no longer belongs to you," Janel stated as she went
back to her stroking motion. "Besides tonight isn't about you, I'm just trying to get my rocks off
and you can go on about the rest of your night. All I ask is that you get this mutha fucker up
and keep it up until I'm done," she demanded. After a few more moments of stroking, I still
wasn't rock solid but it was firm enough to work with. Janel lifted up the short dress that she had on and tore a hole in the leggings she was wearing underneath before grabbing my dick and fed it through the hole right inside of her. Even though I tried not to show it, I was astounded by how wet and warm her pussy was. I mean an easy comparison would be a mini jacuzzi hands
down. I watched as Janel aggressively began to rock back and forth on my dick and digging her
nails into my chest. She seemed to be enjoying herself especially once she felt me get rock
solid inside of her. She kept biting down on her lip which I assumed was to keep herself from
screaming 'cause she was definitely getting her work out on. After a few moments of bull riding,
she started to slow down, and I could feel her legs tighten up, so I pulled her down on top of me
chest to chest. Then I wrapped my arms around her upper body holding her in that position as I

continuously rammed every inch of my dick inside of her as hard, deep, and fast as I could. I

knew she was getting ready to climax. I looked up at her and tears began to roll down her

cheeks and she just couldn't seem to keep her mouth closed.

"Oh....... ah.... oh my God," She moans out as her eyes rolled in the back of her head, she's

about to cum. I keep up with my thunderous strokes up until I hear her screech then I pull her off of me and roll out of the bed. I watched as her body began to shake and she's continuously

climaxing uncontrollably. My job was done so I walked away and hopped in the shower. As the

steaming hot water hit my skin, I couldn't help but to feel bad about what's going on between

Janel and I because Monique is the woman I want to spend the rest of my life with. I put aside

everything including my hoe-ish ways for her, but my hands are tied. Honestly what would you

do if the future between you and the love of your life as well as your freedom were in the hands

of someone else? And walking away isn't an option

(CREATE A K.I.M.)

"Bonjour welcome to Art De' Lamour, how can I help you this evening?" The petite young lady

asked from behind a speaker's podium greeting Monique and I, as we walked through the door.

"Bonjour... and yes you can, we have a reservation for two at ten," Monique said very

theoretically. As I looked around, I couldn't help but notice how exquisite the place looks. The

French doors with gold trim, the huge chandeliers and don't get me started on the beautiful

mosaic pieces they have.

"Name please?" the young lady replied.

"Janel Hudgens," Monique answered. Just the thought of that bitch's name made my skin

crawl, but the look on my baby's face subsided all of that.

"Alright... I have you right here so if you two would be so kind as to follow me right this way I'll

be happy to show you to your seats," the young host insisted so that's exactly what Monique

and I did. We followed the young lady throughout the restaurant and out to the river side

patio. "Here you are, your server will be with you momentarily Avoir," the host added as she

walked away.

"Wow! L.A. honey look at this view," Monique said as she walked over to the French railings,

looking at how the stars and the moon shined so bright against the water. I thought with it being so late and us being so close to the water that it would be extremely cold. But as I took a second look around, I noticed that each glass pillar outside contained an electric double sided fireplace.

"Yeah, it's nice but I have a better view here," I said as I wrapped my hands around her waist. I

gave her a little squeeze as I rested my chin on her collarbone.

"Ah... Bonjour, I am your server for this evening shall I start you all off with drinks?" the server

announced as Monique and I turned around and walked over to our seats.

"Yes, you may... I'm sorry I didn't catch your name," I replied as she handed us our menu.

"Patricia," she kindly responded.

"Well Patricia, I'm driving so I'll have a Sprite, light ice please. And the lady will have a green

Apple Moscato with a shot of V.S.O.P.," I said.

"Okay do you all need a moment to figure out what you want to eat?" Patricia asked.

"No, no... hun I'll have the Shrimp Alfredo with the seawater salmon salad," Monique replied.

"And for you sir?" Patricia questioned.

"Actually, I'm still..."

"He'll have the filet mignon well done with the Alfredo and a baked potato," Monique calmly stated as she intervened.

"Alrighty, I'll go and place your order and I'll be right out with those drinks," Patricia said as she

took the menus and walked off.

"So, you're ordering my food now?" I asked as I gazed into her eyes.

"Yeah, well you ordered my drink. So, consider us even," Monique responded in a joking

manner.

"Yeah okay. This place is truly spectacular though baby," I said.

"Yeah it is, we owe Janel big time for this," she started to say.
"Hey, hey, hey... Let's not talk about anybody else but you and I tonight. Deal?" I asked as
Patricia came by and dropped off the drinks.
"Deal," Monique responded before taking a sip from her drink.
"Hey before it gets too late, I wanna say thank you," I said in a soft tone.
"For what baby?" She asked.
"For being there for my mom, for not leaving my side, and for being my rock when I was at my
lowest," I explained.
"Stop it Frank you're getting me all teary eyed. Baby I thought I had lost you. Seeing all of that
blood all over you and watching you go into shock scared me. And when Dr. Maruchan told
me you had a chance at living I knew then that I wasn't going to leave that hospital without
you. If I had lost you, L.A. it would have been like the devil himself snatching out my soul cause
I really don't know how I would have continued living. That's why I stayed at that hospital day in
and day out. I wasn't going anywhere until you woke up regardless of how long that would
have been," Monique quietly protested.
"Well, I'm here now," I said as I placed my hand over top of hers. Patricia pulls up to the
table with two plates in hand.
"Here you go," she said as she placed the plates in front of Monique then turning her attention
to me. "Yours should be up shortly," she added before walking away.
"You want me to wait?" Monique questioned as she laid her napkin across her lap.

"Nah baby go ahead enjoy. Hey, I like the dress you have on by the way, I don't think I've seen

you in that one before, is that new?" I questioned.

"Actually, I wore this dress the first night we went to dinner in Paris. And maybe you don't

remember seeing me in it sir, because you were so focused on getting me out of it," she

quickly replied as she cut a piece of salmon and ate it with the Shrimp Alfredo.

"Now that my love just might be true," I responded, causing both of us to laugh.

"Here you are sir," Patricia said as she approached the table and presented me with my food.

"Is there anything else I can get for you two?" Patricia asked.

"No, not at the moment" Monique dismissingly said.

"Someone's being a little mean," I added in a joking manner.

"Yeah, well she interrupted an important conversation we were having," Monique replied.

"Oh yeah, and what conversation is that?" I asked.

"A convo on whether or not you were planning on helping me out of this dress again or do I have to do it myself?" She countered.

"Ummmmm I'll think about it," I teasingly said as I took a bite out of my steak.

"Oh, I see you wanna play games tonight. That's cool, I bet you'll have your mind made up by

the time we get home," Monique insisted.

"And if I don't?" I asked.

"Trust me you will," she answered. Monique and I rambled on for about another hour or so and

as I gazed into her eyes it felt like Paris all over again. And even though everything that happened leading up to this moment was painful and life changing I would do it all again just to

have this moment.

"I'm sorry to interrupt, but here's your check," Patricia said as she placed the black leather

tablet on the table and started to walk away.

"Hey Patricia....quick question for you. Why do they call this place Art De' L'amour?" Monique

asked as she took a sip from her now third glass of Moscato. So, by now she should have a

slight buzz.

"Well, the owner is actually from France and so are the cooks here. The French people use a

natural aphrodisiac when cooking their foods. As you know aphrodisiacs are meant to

stimulate you and put you in the mood to make love hence the name Art De' L'amour which

means 'The Art of Love'," Patricia kindly explained.

"So basically, if she's all hot and bothered, it's because she's been drugged?" I asked.

"No, no, dear God no! They just use natural spices that ultimately heightens your sexual desire

or drive. So, if either of you were feeling a little frisky before dinner this evening then someone

may be getting lucky tonight," Patrica replied with a slight chuckle. Monique and I just looked at

each other and laughed as Patricia walked away with the remaining dishes.

"Wow this place actually wasn't as expensive as I thought it would be," I said looking over the

bill.

"Let me see," Monique said as she started to reach across the table.

"Nah baby don't worry about this. You just take this twenty and have the valet grab the car I'll

be out in a second," I suggested.

"Yes Sir! Oh, and make sure you leave that young lady a nice tip," Monique said as she stood

up.

"I thought you didn't like her," I responded in a joking manner.

"Oh, shut up, she was just doing her job. Besides, she was a very good server tonight. So

leave her a good tip." She replied as she walked up to the front of the restaurant.

"I always do," I said. As I watched Monique disappear out of sight, I noticed Patricia

approaching so I stood up and grabbed the leather tablet that contained the check as well as

the payment inside. "Here you go," I said as I handed her the tablet then grabbing two

hundred dollars out of my wallet to give Patricia before continuing. "And this is for you, your

hospitality was excellent tonight," I added.

"Anytime sweetheart," Patrica said as she put the money inside her apron and handed

me a card from Art De' L'amour with a handwritten number on the back with her name next to

it. "Call me, sometime," she added.

"Yeah, I'm sorry Patricia but that won't be happening. If you didn't notice the ring earlier. That

woman I was with is my fiancé. Plus, you're only like what seventeen.... eighteen?" I asked.

"Actually, I just turned twenty," she calmly responded.

"Not much of a difference. Babygirl you're still young," I replied as I tried handing her back the card.

"Nah, keep it," she protested.

"I'm engaged," I stated once more.

"Right not married," she quickly responded as she calmly walked off. As I walked up to the

front of the restaurant, I had a choice to make. Either tell Monique about what had just transpiredand deal with her possibly wanting to fuck the little girl up or just not say anything and continue on with my beautiful night. I tossed the card in the trash can outside before I got in the car.

"Honey what took you so long," Monique asked.

"Ah... nothing, I just asked Patricia to let the chef know that the food was amazing," I answered

as we pulled off.

"Oh okay. Hey. Let's play truth or dare," Monique suggested.

"Baby really? What are we sixteen, seventeen again?" I asked.

"No..... We are two adults having some fun. But I mean if you're scared, I understand," she said

taunting me.

"Okay whatever. You start," I submissively replied.

"Yay okay. Truth or dare" she asked.

"Truth." I answered.

"Is it true that I'm getting some tonight?" she asked.

"That would be false. My turn. Truth or dare?" I answered then asked.

"You petty. Dare," She answered.

"Ummmm... ah.... oh, okay I dare you to kiss me," I stated.

"Where?" Monique asked as she began to seductively bite down on her thumb nail.

"My cheek, woman.! My cheek!" I said. She leaned across the center console and gave me a

five second kiss on my cheek.

"Truth or Dare?" she asked and for most of the ride I kept picking truth and she would ask me

questions like why do I love her? What makes her special? Baby names and all kinds of sexual

fantasies. About ten minutes away from the house for whatever reason I racked up the balls to

say "Dare" and as soon as the words rolled off my tongue, I regretted it.

"For the next five minutes regardless to what I do you have to continue driving and you cannot

move either of your hands off of the steering wheel," Monique demanded.

"Ha, nope! Game over," I said as I laughed.

"Well, you can say no all you want, you picked dare now you have to live with the

consequences," she responded as she lifted up the center console and laid across the seat with her head facing me and she started to unzip my pants.

"Monique I said, no," I tried saying it without a smile on my face.

"You can say no as many times as you want but the fact still remains you picked dare and

there's not much you can do to stop me when you're driving anyways," she argued as she pulled out my dick.

"I'm sure this is some form of rape," I protested.

"Well if you still want to go to the police station in the morning and file a report I'll be glad to

take you, until then shhh," Monique commanded as she ran her tongue all around my dick

like it was a Mr. Softy ice cream cone before wrapping her juicy lips around my mic. I'm only able to watch her slowly swallow my dick for a few seconds before the red light turns green. Not

being able to watch made the touch of her lips and tongue much more sensitive than usual.

"Baby, hold up a second a police officer is pulling up on the side of us!" I said as I tried to look as normal as possible, and I thought she would have quickly sat up and put her seatbelt on but no. Monique maintained her position and at one point even shoved every inch of my dick down her throat forcing me to maintain a calm composure. She's doing such a good job I can already feel my legs getting weak. The cops drove right past me after cruising alongside us for about a mile.

"You must be really trying to go to jail tonight?" I asked.

"Am I getting some tonight?" she countered after slowly pulling my dick out of her mouth.

"Yes baby, I've had plans on diving inside of you. I just wanted you to beg for it. Now will

you stop so I can get us home safely. We are right up the street see.," I said as I pointed out

the window. Monique sat up and wiped the cum off her mouth. "So, you just gone leave me

hangin' out like this?" I asked.

"Might as well, I'm going to pick up where I left off at once we get inside since you don't want me to finish now.," she said as she firmly gripped my dick causing my knee to jerk and my foot to

press down on the gas slightly harder. Many thoughts began to rush through my mind about

what I planned on doing to her and it was crazy. Even though we were only down the street,

getting there seemed to take FOREVER. We finally pulled up into the driveway.

"Wait right here! " I said as I jumped out of the car and went to open up the front door then

rushed back over to her side of the car.

"Mmmm what's this?" she asked as I pulled her out of the car then picked her up. Monique wrapped her legs around me as I carried her in the house. As soon as we crossed that

threshold and closed the door it was on and poppin'. With her legs still wrapped around me we

started passionately kissing I turned around and rammed her back into the front door as she

slowly peeled off the jacket to my Armani two-piece suit. Multiple kisses were being exchanged

all over our neck and collarbone as she ripped open my button-down shirt. I eased down

her panties. I hiked up her dress and since I never fixed myself from the previous enjoyment in

the car reaching for my dick was fairly easy. Monique wrapped her arms around my neck

moaning in my ear as I slowly eased my dick inside of her tender and succulent pussy. The

deeper I went, the more I felt her nails digging into my shoulder blades. After about twenty

minutes of drilling Monique up against the front door, I felt my legs start to become weary from

the extra weight I was supporting, and even though Monique isn't a big girl, my injuries still

prevented me from doing certain things. I carry her over a few steps and sit her on top of the

coffee table, I leaned her back against the wall and helped her pull off her dress all while still

balls deep inside of her. I watched her as she's looking down watching my dick disappear and

reappear with every stroke as she's holding onto my waist. Watching her facial expressions

only motivated me to stroke harder and a little faster. Once I pick up the pace I watch as

Monique uses one hand to rub on her clit and the other to play with and squeeze her titties. I feel her warm cum sliding down my dick as I'm stroking then once she finished cumming I feel her hand pressing against my abdomen.

"Wait..." she said, causing me to slowly pull out. She climbed down off the coffee table and

unbuckled my belt pulling my pants and boxers down before pushing me up against the table.

Monique slowly dropped down to her knees and leaving her hands behind her back she veiled

her lips around my dick passionately cleaning up her mess she had previously made. I looked

down and all I see is just her head going crazy and a small puddle of saliva forming on my hard

wood floors.

"Damn...." I said once the oral pleasure finally stopped. Monique stood up with a grin on her

face as she wiped the corners of her mouth and grabbed my hand guiding me over to the living

room and pushed me down onto the couch. As she was getting ready to get on top of me and

ride, I stopped her.

"What?" she asked as if something was wrong.

"Nothing.... I'm just thirsty," I said as I pulled her closer to my head region. I grabbed her left

leg and placed it on my right side before pulling her down on top of my face. I laid back on that

couch and consumed almost every drop of her sweet and succulent pussy as if I was the more sexy and seductive version of the Cookie Monster. I was determined to make her continuously climax and each time she came she tried to run but like a vampire feeding I just couldn't get enough. It was like each time she came her pussy kept getting sweeter and sweeter. Monique finally escapes my hold and slides right down on top of my dick. She lightly drags her nails across my chest as she rocks just her bottom half back and forth. Her rocking starts getting quicker as she took off her bra then leaned over allowing me to lick and suck all over her beautiful soft titties.

"Oh my god, I love you so much," Monique moaned out as I held her close to me consistently

feeding her pussy ardent strokes. She sat straight up after a few fulfilling strokes and I watched

as her body quivered while she came. Holding her hands behind her head as if she was being

detained I sat up and positioned myself in the middle of the couch while still inside of her. As

Monique grabbed a hold to the back of the couch; I could feel myself getting to that tipping point. I slid down off the couch to the floor onto my knees as I laid Monique down in front of me. I kissed her all over her neck, shoulders and chest before sliding back inside of her tight wet pussy as her fingers ran through my hair before scratchin me up. As I continued to thrust deeper and deeper, I couldn't help but to get lost inside of her eyes as I gazed upon her beauty. The only thing that kept running through my mind was the fact that if I died right now, she would have nothing to remember me by.

"You love me?" I asked as my strokes became more forceful.

"YES!" she moaned out.

"I'm bouta cum," I said as my forceful thrusts became quicker.

"Mmmmm I want it all over my titties," she replied as she began to play with her nipples. I

cradled her head in the palm of my hand as I continued my fluent motion.

"Nah.... I want you to have my baby," I said, feeling my pipe getting ready to burst. Monique never offered a response to my statement nor did she seem reluctant at all to the idea of my

proposal. And as I was cumming I noticed a tear creep down the side of her face and in a way I

felt like our bodies had connected on a deeper level. The grin on Monique's face was a real

moment of relief for me as I rolled off of her and onto the floor next to her. We both laid there out of breath and extremely satisfied. Monique rolled over onto her side swinging her left leg across

me.

"That was amazing," she protested as she fondled my hair.

"Yeah, tell me about it." I quickly responded.

-BOOM-BOOM-BOOM-.

"You expecting someone?" Monique asked after we both sat up to see what the loud thumps

were at the door.

"No... nah I'm not," I responded as I jumped to my feet and walked over to the door after

grabbing one of my pistols out of the closet and racked it. "Who is it?" I shouted through the

front door. Monique tossed me my pants as I motioned for her to go to the bedroom.

"It's us boss, open up we need to talk," the voice on the other side of the door said. It sounded

like Tae but with me being unsure I brought the pistol up to eye level as I opened the door.

"L.A. who is it?" Monique yelled out.

"It's just the fellas baby," I responded before turning my attention back to the door. "What's up

fellas come on in," I finished. Tae, Jay-Money and J.T. all walked into my house with stern looks of frustration on their faces. I looked down at my watch and it's almost a quarter after

1a.m. "So, what's so important fellas that it couldn't wait?" I asked. They all looked at each

other but only one spoke out.

"L.A. man I'm sorry if we interrupted you tonight but you asked us to dig up some info. Well

the streets been talking, and word is one of Trigga's boys spotted you earlier last night and

Trigga is planning on finishing you off tonight," Tae explained.

"Oh yeah?" I questioned.

"Yeah L.A. forget about all of that clean shit you talkin' 'bout, we gotta go get this nigga before

he gets you," J.T. stepped in and added.

"Do any of y'all even know where this nigga at?" I asked as we all gathered around the dinning

room table.

"Yeah, he at his crib over on Blake and fourth," Jay-Money chimed in and said as I poured up a

shot of Patron.

"How you know he's still there?" I questioned after throwing back a shot.

"We got BO sitting at his house right now, I told him to shot me code 16-21-14 when he's on

the move," J.T. said.

"Yeah, so once we know he's on the move we can catch his bitch ass in traffic," Jay-Money

announced as he pulled out a 3-57. "Yeah, no casings," he added.

"Nah if we gone do this, we gone catch him where he lay his muthafucking head," I stated.

"But his girl and nephew live there with him," Tae said as if he had a hint of worry in his voice.

"And what does that mean? That nigga don't care about who I might be with when he comes for

me, so why should I?" I replied in a more elevated tone.

" L.A. everything's alright honey?" Monique called out from the bedroom.

"Yeah, baby everything's good," I answered.

"So how we gone do this?" Jay-Money asked.

"You still got that machete?" I pointed at J.T. questioning.

"Yeah, why what's up?" J.T. countered.

"Y'all go strap up, guns, gloves, wear all black and meet me over on Trimble and fourth. J.T.

bring that machete and y'all make sure don't shit have a single print on it," I commanded as the

fellas and I made our way to the front door.

"When is this going down?! " Tae asked. Jay-Money and J.T. just looked at him as if he had to

be the slowest person they had ever met.

"It should have been going down twenty minutes ago to be honest so go suit up and meet me

on Trimble and fourth in twenty minutes," I responded as I opened the door to let them out.

"Alright fellas let's go," J.T. said to both Jay-Money and Tae before turning his attention to

me. "Hey, I'll blow down on BO on my way there to let him know what's up so that he can keep

a look out," J.T. added.

"Good I'll holla at y'all in a minute," I said as I closed my door then made my way back to my

room. I was so caught up in my own head I didn't even say a word to Monique as I walked into

the room.

"Everything okay?" Monique asked as she saw me getting dressed. I threw on one of my all

black Nike jogging fits with the checkered black on black timbs; never once offering Monique a

response. Once I sat on the edge of the bed to lace up my boots Monique threw a pillow at the

back of my head snapping me back to reality. "Frank!" she shouted.

"What...What's up baby?" I asked as I pulled out a black duffel bag and began looking for a

few items.

"What's going on?" Monique questioned looking paranoid as she watched me go to my safe

and pull out five thousand dollars.

"Listen to me my love and listen good, without any back talk or questions. I want you to pack

your suitcase with some clothes for tonight. You're going to take this money and the Cadillac and drive out to Wixom. I want you to go to this hotel called Brushy Creek. Once you're there you're going to ask for the overnight manager named Deondray. When he comes out ask to speak with him in private and let him know that I sent you. You're going to give him a thousand dollars and he's going to put you up in a suite that I already have the number to, and you will wait for my call on the cell phone that he will give you. If you think you are being followed don't panic just continue on course and once you get up to the room check under the nightstand by the bed there will be a 9mm just like this one," I said as I tossed mine from my hip onto the bed before going on. "Grab it, make sure the safety is off and don't open that door for no one. Got it?!" I asked. Monique never opened her mouth to give me a verbal answer, but she did shake her head in confirmation. "Let's go baby grab ya stuff," I added as I grabbed my cleaning kit from the closet and broke down the 9mm to clean it. Monique hurried out of the bed without any questions or back talk and started to pack her bags. Once I made sure the gun and bullets were clean, I went back to the closet and grabbed my nightstick special ops edition and cleaned the

prints off of that as well. I threw the nightstick as well as a few other items into the duffle bag

then put the 9mm back on my hip. I threw on my black Polo hoodie and I was all set to go,"

Baby, are you ready?" I asked as I made my way to the front door. A moment of silence crept

through the house briefly before I finally saw Monique come out of the bedroom and walk down

the hall with her suitcase and purse in hand. "You ready?" I questioned. All Monique did was

shake her head in confirmation, but once I reached to open the door, she stepped in front of me.

"I love you L.A.," Monique said as she gazed into my eyes.

"I love you too baby," I said as I caressed the side of her face wiping away the tears that began

to fall down her cheek.

"Promise me two things," she stated.

"What's up?" I asked.

"Promise me you're coming home to me. And that this ends today," Monique answered.

"I promise you that I'ma try and make it home to you. But one thing for certain and two things

for sure regardless of how it ends.... This ends TODAY!" I replied. Monique dropped her purse

and her suitcase and wrapped her arms around me. We shared a few kisses then out the door

we went. I watched as she got into the Cadillac and drove off in the opposite direction as me, then I pulled off. As I made my way to our predetermined destination, I couldn't help but to think

about my life and everything that I have been through and prevailed. Whereas most people

would have allowed their circumstances to break them. Then I thought about what my dad used

to say.

"Son... tough times don't last, tough people do." When I was a child, I could never understand

why he said that to me but once I got older, I realized that he was not only talking about being

physically strong but more importantly being mentally strong as well. "You protect yourself and

the ones you love by all means," he'd used to say, and tonight will be no different from any other times that I have had to. I pulled up to corner of Trimble and fourth and waited J.T and the fellas pulled up alongside of me.

"Who ride is that?" I asked as I rolled down my window noticing that the ride was pretty damn

nice.

"Aw man one of the junkies I be serving got like his own used car lot so every week I'm on

something new," Jay-Money explained.

"Oh, okay so...What's the status?" I questioned.

"Well, we just had BO do a walk by and he said that there is no one on the main floor. Trigga

and his bitch sleep upstairs. Trigga's nephew sleeps in the basement so how you wanna do

this?" J.T. asked.

"You and Jay-Money come with me through the front and Tae you go through the back. Once in J.T., you and Tae quietly go and grab the nephew and bring him up to the top floor where

Jay-Money and I will be with Trigga and his bitch. Got it?" I asked.

"Yup... let's go," they all replied. I followed them up to Trigga's spot since I didn't know exactly

where his house was. We pulled up and the fellas hopped out with their ski masks and gloves on, guns in hand ready for war. I grabbed the duffle bag out of the backseat then joined the group. As planned Tae went through the back yard to go through the back while Jay-Money and I watched J.T. pick the lock on the front door.

"Got it," J.T. quietly said as he slowly opened the door. Trigga's house was designed as an

open concept house so as we entered, we could see Tae coming in through the back at the

same time. Once we were in, as planned J.T. broke off to go help Tae retrieve Trigga's nephew, while Jay-Money and I made our way upstairs. Jay-Money and I carefully opened up every door

that we passed and found nothing up until we got to the end of the hall. Jay-Money slowly

eased the door open with his gun drawn. I saw Trigga and his bitch laying there in the bed, I

slowly walked over to his side of the bed while Jay-Money stood at the end of the bed aiming his gun at Trigga and his bitch. Before waking him up, I checked underneath the nightstand and in

the drawer for any weapons.

"Wake up bitch," I said as I backhanded the shit out of him then took a step back. Trigga

awakened with a ball of multiple emotions on his face. The first was shock which I assumed came from the bitch smack to the face. The second emotion was fear. Fear of not knowing who was in his home. The last emotion was vulnerability. That moment when he realized exactly who he was fucking with. Trigga quickly rolled over to reach for his gun. "Nah I already got that," I added as Jay-Money popped on the light. All of Trigga's extra moves woke his lady.

"Baby what's wrong.... Oh.... Oh my god!" she screamed out as she quickly grabbed ahold of

Trigga.

"It's okay baby," Trigga said to his lady before turning his attention to me. "Look L.A. ya beef is

with me man why don't you just let her go," he added as he held on to his chick to comfort her.

"Get up!" I demanded as I pulled out my gun and aimed it at his chest. "Tie him up," I turned

and told Jay-Money as I tossed him the duffle bag. Trigga slowly climbed out of the bed and

began to walk past me.

"Get the fuck over here," Jay-Money said as he snatched Trigga up by the collar of his shirt

yanking him over to the center of the room.

"Look who we found, Boss," Tae said as he and J.T. brought in Trigga's nephew that was in the

basement and put him on his knees.

"Tie him up too," I said before turning my attention to the young lady, "Come here," I added

extending my index finger back and forth as if calling for a child to come closer.

"Don't you dare touch her!" Trigga yelled out from his knees.

"Hey Tae, do me a favor and tape his fucking mouth shut," I said before turning my attention

back to the young lady in the bed. "What's your name?" I asked.

"Amber." she responded all shaken up.

"Hold on one second Amber," I said as I turned my focus over to the fellas. "J.T., Tae search the room for his safe, I know it's up here. Ain't that right Trigga, see some things never change.

You were always one to keep ya money close to you," I said before turning back to Amber. "Alright sweetheart this is how this is going to go. I ask a question. And you answer it. You will

not lie to me, you will not try to stall in hopes of finding a way out of this situation. Cause I'll let

you know now it's only two ways out of this... Dead and useless or Alive and helpful. I want

you to let that sink in for a moment, and just let me know when you're ready to answer your first

question," I explained as Tae and J.T. tore Trigga's master suite apart.

"I'm ready," Amber replied after looking over at Trigga.

"Good, question number one is easy. How long have you been with Trigga?" I asked.

"A little over six years now. But we have only been married for five years," she answered.

"Hey L.A. I think we got something, this wall sounds hollow," J.T. called out from across the

room.

"Bust it out!" I responded before getting back to Amber. "Now, Amber honey, this next

question will be a little harder. What is the combination?" I asked.

"Got it boss," Tae called out confirming that what they had come across was in fact Trigga's

safe.

"I don't know the combination," Amber answered. I looked over at Trigga who was making loud

noises as if he had something to say, so I gave Jay-Money a nod and he removed the tape

that covered Trigga's mouth.

"Baby, you don't need to tell him shit. He wants me not you; he's just trying to scare it out of
you cause he knows he ain't getting shit out of me," Trigga shouted before I gave Jay-Money the cue to shut him the fuck up. Both J.T. and Tae rejoined the group as Jay-Money placed the tape back over Trigga's mouth.
"Now Amber I'm going to ask you once again, what is the combination to the safe?" I asked in
a very stern tone. A moment of silence filled the room and right when I thought Amber would
make the smart choice she just remained silent. "Hey J.T. did you bring what I told you to
bring?" I asked.
"Yeah," he answered as he pulled the machete out of the duffle bag and handed it to me. I knocked off the lamp and the house phone that sat on top of the nightstand
and dragged the waist high nightstand over to the end of the bed.
"Stand up!" I demanded as I pointed at Trigga's nephew. Trigga's nephew complied with my
demand. "What's ya name son?" I asked as I walked over and untied the rope from around
his hands.
"Tyson," the kid hesitantly responded.
"Alright Tyson, do me a favor and place your right hand on the table and spread your fingers for
me?" I asked.
"Oh my God, no what are you going to do to him!?" Amber shouted as she crawled to the end
of the bed.
"It's okay auntie," Tyson said reassuring Amber.
"Oh shit! We got a family that got some heart. That's what's up I guess," I said as I waved the

machete around in the air. "And you're sure you don't know the combination to the safe?" I
turned and asked Amber yet still no response. "Well, you can't say I didn't try to be reasonable,"
I added before bringing down a striking blow with the machete severing Tyson's hand from his
arm. All three of them either screamed or yelled once they saw blood shooting out
everywhere. "Now that I have your attention. In less than five minutes Tyson here will die
from loss of blood, but I'm only giving you two minutes to give me the fucking code or I'm going
to chop off his other hand!" I said as I held the bloody machete to Amber's face. Amber sat
there in awe watching Tyson struggle to stop the bleeding. She was definitely in a trance.
"Don't tell him shit.!" Tyson mustered up some strength to speak.
"You know what... Times up!" I said as I drove the machete right through Tyson's heart.
"Noooooo!!!" Amber yelled out in tears as she jumped from the bed and crawled over to
Tyson's lifeless body.
"No, no, no.... Get up!" I demanded grabbing Amber by her hair snatching her up to her feet as I continued. "Now for some odd reason Trigga seems to think that this is a fucking game and he
has talked you into believing the same thing, but now as you both can see shit just got real.
He's going to DIE! understand that? Now it's up to you whether you live or fulfill that 'till death do us part' quote in your vows," I explained before dragging her over to the other side of the room
to the safe. "What the fuck is the combination to this muthafucking safe Bitch! And this the last

time I'm going to ask you!" I shouted as I threw her to the floor, pulled out my gun and aimed it

at the back of her head. Amber looked back at Trigga as if she wanted approval and after about

a minute Trigga nodded his head giving her the signal she was looking for. Very shaken up

Amber started to punch in the seven-digit combination to open the safe. "Amber, Amber,

Amber.... Why did you lie to me?" I asked as the door of the safe popped open.

"I figured if you all couldn't get into the safe y'all would just leave," she responded.

"Hey fellas what's the two main things that I absolutely hate?" I asked.

"A liar and a thief," they all said.

"Look at Trigga," I said as I pointed in his direction. "See, I'm not sure if you know this or not but

Trigga here used to work for me. I would even go as far as saying I'm the reason he even has a

name in this game. Would you agree?" I asked as I motioned for Jay-Money to remove the tape

again.

"L.A. look you made your point man, and you got what you wanted so just leave," Trigga

pleaded once Jay-Money removed the tape as a tear ran down his face.

"No, see that's where you're wrong. I came for you. But answer me this real quick, you were

there when Darius lied to me about my money right?" I asked. Trigga wouldn't give a verbal

answer he just shook his head. "You remember what I did to him?" I questioned. Trigga once

again, didn't give a verbal response he just put his head down. "Point is Amber, I HATE A

FUCKING LIAR!" I added as I struck her with the butt of the gun putting her right to sleep.

"Amber NO! You son of a bitch. Are you that much of a pussy that you would hurt a

woman?" Trigga angrily asked.

"You shot me over some bullshit that I had nothing to do with," I said before switching my

focus. "Tae, hogtie this bitch. J.T. go turn on the water in the bathroom to fill up the tub," I

commanded.

"Your right hand mans killed my cousin and his friends L.A. you already know how it is in these

streets, blood for blood," Trigga pleaded.

"But Trigga I came to you once I found out that the kid he killed was your people and you told

me out of your own damn mouth that everything was good. So basically, you lied to me and

caught me slippin right? And speaking of the streets I heard you was planning on getting at

me again cause one of ya little homeboys saw me out last night. You didn't think I would get

wind of that cause I ain't out here in these streets as deep as I used to be huh?" I asked. Trigga

just sat there silent as he watched Tae finish hogtying his wife, Amber.

"Hey L.A., the tub is full," J.T. said as he stood in the doorway of the bathroom.

"Good, come help Tae get this bitch over in it!" I ordered as I stepped over her body to get to

the safe. The safe was full of money and drugs. "Oh, shit boys look what we got here," I said

as I started to toss the stacks and stacks of money along with what looked to be crystal meth onto the bed. "You been out here getting a little money I see," I added as I emptied out the

safe and Jay-Money packed everything into their duffle bag.

"Hey, boss this chick is starting to wake up," Tae called out from the bathroom.

"See Trigga now it's a party," I said as I walked towards the master bathroom after grabbing my

taser out of my duffle bag. I walked into the master bathroom and saw J.T. and Tae standing

over Amber who sat sideways in the tub full of what I assumed to be cold water since she was

shivering so hard

"I'm so sorry... I'm sorry I lied to you.... just please don't hurt me." Amber pleaded as tears

continuously ran down her face.

"Jay-Money.... go ahead and bring him in here," I called out. Jay-Money brought Trigga into the

master bathroom and sat him down on the toilet across from the tub. I kneeled down next to the

tub and moved her hair out of her face. "To be honest with you Amber I didn't plan on causing

harm to you or your nephew but you lying to me forced my hand. And I'm not sure why Trigga

would encourage you to continue to be dishonest with me knowing that I really, really hate being lied to," I explained as I stood up.

"I'm sorry L.A.... really I am, but you don't have to do this," Amber stated.

"You're right Amber I don't, you're going to do it to yourselves. I replied.

"What do you mean?" Amber questioned.

"I have a math problem in my head that I want answered and the first one of you to answer it correctly won't get shot," I said as I nodded my head and Jay-Money for the last time removed

the tape. I took a moment and looked at both Trigga and Amber with a devilish smile on my face. "What is three to the second power minus two plus fourteen, divided by seven?" I

questioned. Trigga looked at Amber with sadness in his eyes and Amber had the same loom in

her eyes and right when I thought both of them would hold their tongue and not speak.

"Three ... The answer is three," Amber shouted.

"That's correct, and see I'm glad that you answered cause it makes this a lot easier," I said as I

turned on the taser and dropped it into the tub with Amber.

"NOOO!!! you hoe ass bitch!" Trigga cried out as he watched Amber's body began to jolt and

tremble inside of the tub. That taser I dropped in that tub held enough voltage to kill a horse so in a matter of moments she was dead.

"What? I didn't lie right? I said that the first person to answer it correctly wouldn't get shot,

and as you can see, she didn't get shot," I said.

"You knew she would answer the question, even if I would have answered it you would have

still killed her just to make me watch her die," Trigga replied.

"See fellas, I told y'all he wasn't as stupid as he looks. You're right, regardless to who would

have answered the question I still would have killed the lying bitch first to ensure you suffer," I

responded.

"Why?" Trigga simply asked.

"Because of you, at the end of the day Trigga it was either going to be me or you. I couldn't come here and try to squash the beef with you again and allow you to rock me to sleep.

Besides I promised my wife that regardless of how this would go down, this shit ends today," I

quickly answered.

"So, what now you expect me to sit here and beg you not to kill me?" Trigga questioned as he

stood up. "Cause I'm not!" he added.

"If I thought for one second that this was going to go down like that then that would have took

all the fun out of it for me," I answered as I aimed the pistol to Trigga's head.

"Hey L.A. man why don't you let me have a go at him before you lay him down," J.T.

interrupted and spoke out. I looked over at J.T. who was putting on a pair of brass knuckles,

looked back over at Trigga then just walked out of the bathroom and sat down on the edge of

the bed. Over the next few minutes all I heard was punches being landed and sounds of pain and agony. Then after a few more moments the cries of pain stopped. Jay-Money and Tae hauled Trigga out of the bathroom tossing him to the floor at my feet, and seconds later J.T. came walking out with a towel in hand wiping the blood off of his gloves and brass knuckles. Trigga laid there in front of me on the floor with multiple contusions and cuts all over his face. and judging by how bad he was curled up in the fetal position I could tell he had a few broken ribs as well.

"I see you worked up a bit of a sweat," I said to J.T. as he made his way closer to me.

"He..... he hits like a bitch," Trigga struggled to say as if his jaw was broken before he spat out

blood in J.T.'s direction and we all laughed.

"See, typically, I would tell you to watch your mouth but seeing as though you're a dead man

anyway, I'll just count that as part of your last words," I stated as I grabbed my gun off of the

bed beside me screwing on a silencer before continuing. "Anyways anything else you want to

say?" I asked as I aimed the gun at his forehead.

"Yeah," Trigga said before going silent.

"Alright well spit it out, I ain't got all day," I said breaking the silence that had once filled the

room.

"I'll see you in hell, Bitch," Trigga shouted before I pulled the trigger.

"You guys take what you want, make it look like a robbery gone wrong. Be out of here in five

minutes," I commanded as I stepped over Trigga's lifeless body that laid on the floor in front of

me.

(CREATE A BLANK PAGE FOR K.I.M. TO BE PUT IN LATER)

As I am driving through Wixom, I finally come across the Brushy Creek hotel that L.A. was
talking about. I pulled into the parking lot, parked then made my way into the fancy hotel.

"Hello, welcome to Brushy Creeks, my name is Sam. How can I help you?" The young lady
behind the counter asked.

"Yes, by any chance is your night manager Deondray working tonight?" I countered.

"Actually, he is, I'll grab him for you. Just wait here for a moment," Sam responded as she
walked off. I took a look around to be sure that I wasn't being followed.

"Hey, I'm Deondray, how can I help you?" he asked as he walked out with Sam by his side.

"Yeah, hey Deondray, is it possible I can speak with you in private?" I questioned.

"Yeah sure.... Follow me," Deondray answered as he walked me over to the seating area in the
lobby. We both sat down across from each other and there was a peculiar jiffy of silence. "So
how can I help you?" Deondray asked once more.

"L.A. sent me," I replied. Deondray's eyes got bigger once he allowed what was just said to
set in.

"Follow me!" he responded as he stood up and sprang into action. We walked back over to the
front desk and Deondray disappeared behind the counter. Once he came back into view and
from behind the desk, I noticed that he had a room key and a cell phone in his hands. We

walked over to the elevator, got on and rode it up to the top floor. We walked down the hall and

entered the first door on the left. Once there Deondray gave me the room key as well as the

phone that was in his hands. "Don't open this door for anyone," he reminded me closing the

door as he left. As soon as he closed the door, I rushed over to the bedroom to check

underneath the nightstand and just like L.A. said there was a standard 9mm inside a holster

taped under the nightstand. I looked around the room as I flopped down on the bed. My brain

began to hurt just thinking about what could go wrong and what L.A. was out there doing so I

decided to take a bath to soothe my nerves. I get up and went to the bathroom to turn on the

hot water. While I looked through my suitcase trying to find something to put on once I got out.

Once my bath is done being drawn, I climbed out of my clothes and positioned myself at the edge of the tub as I slid in. After about thirty minutes of soaking in that hot water my nerves finally started to relax, so I laid back and closed my eyes. The first person I could picture was L.A. I thought about the future we are building and how much my world has been impacted

ever since he came back into my life. Both my father and my brother were taken away

from me and without L.A. by my side, I'm not sure how I would be able to get through this pain.

Every day that I wake up I start to feel that loneliness and vacancy in my heart and right when

I'm at my breaking point L.A. saves me each and every time. At first, I wasn't sure if he was ready to give up his hoe-ish ways and street lifestyle, but over the course of these last ten months L.A.

has truly shown me that with me is where he wants to be. I start to feel the water in the tub

begin to cool down after another forty-five minutes, I looked at the cell phone I was given as I got out of the tub and wrapped a dry towel around me and nothing. Not a missed call or a

text, NOTHING! and naturally I begin to worry all over again. I laid across the bed in my towel

holding the cell phone hoping to hear something from L.A., But all there ended up being was

silence. It was so silent I could hear the sound of the elevator door opening up and footsteps

walking down the halls. I looked over at the door and I saw the shadow of the footsteps I was

hearing, had stopped right outside my door. So, I rolled over and grabbed the pistol from the

nightstand and aimed it at the door. I heard the sound of a key card being accepted then the

doorknob turned. My heart begins to race watching as the door eased open, but it was L.A. A

shot of relief cruised through my body once I noticed it was him.

"Baby, is everything okay? I thought you were going to call," I stated as I got off the bed and

rushed towards him, but he was silent. The closer I got I could see the small blood spatters all

over his face. "Come on baby stand right here. Let's get you out of these clothes and into the

shower," I added. L.A. just stood there as if he was daydreaming while I carefully removed every article of clothing off of his body. After I stripped him down to just his boxers and socks, I

walked him into the bathroom turned on the water in the walk-in shower then finished removing

what clothing he had left. When he stepped into the shower he just stood under the hot water

with his head down. I couldn't stand to see my baby like this, so I unknotted my towel and

stepped inside the shower with him. I grabbed a dry face towel off the hook outside the

shower, wet it, and gently wiped the blood off of his face. Holding his face in the palm of my

hands. I couldn't help but to look into his eyes and it was as if I was looking in the eyes of a man I had never seen before. I wasn't one hundred percent sure what he had done or how far things

had gone, all I know is as long as I'm with him I will always be safe. Tonight, has truly shown me that he will do whatever's necessary to protect the ones he loves, even if that means becoming

someone he has tried so hard to put away. "Hey.... hey look at me.... it's over. You hear me?

Honey it's over," I said in a very soft tone. As I continued to look into his eyes, I could see L.A.

The L.A. that I fell in love with was starting to come back to me. As my lips touched his I felt his arms wrap around me. He took a few steps back and sat down on the shower bench.

"I love you," L.A. whispered into my ear as I sat down on his lap.

"I love you too baby," I responded and the next thing I knew I felt my feet leave the ground and

my back slammed into the shower wall under the shower head. I started to feel the touch of his

soft lips on my neck then my chest. I wrapped my arms around his neck as I felt his dick slowly divide the lips of my soft moist pussy. L.A. and I continued making out and as soon as I

wrapped my legs around his waist I begin to feel his thick succulent dick penetrate my tight,

wet walls. While giving me some big ass hickies all over my neck and titties, I feel him slowly

stroking deeper and deeper inside of me and my God he feels so good. Once he felt my legs

tighten up he knew I was getting ready to cum, so his strokes became hastier and abysmal

until I climaxed all over his stern dick. Once L.A. released me from his grip, I put my hand in the

middle of his chest as I pushed him back to the shower bench and sat him down. I slowly

squatted down while running my hands along the sides of L.A.'s thighs before finally gripping his dick with both hands. While looking into his eyes, I took one lick then another before eventually

easing every inch of him that I could take to the back of my throat. You could have sworn I was

trying to find out how many licks it takes to get the center of his lollipop by the way I worked my

tongue and lips around his dick and I still wanted more; but then I felt his hand grab a fist full of

my hair pulling me back up to eye level. "I wasn't done, papi," I moaned out as we effortlessly

traded places.

"I know," L.A. said as he kneeled down. "Daddy's thirsty," he added as he pulled me down to

the edge of the bench and placed one of my legs on his shoulder while propping the other in the air against the shower glass. In the matter of seconds, I feel the grace of his long, thick, and plentiful tongue separates the lips of my pussy. L.A. began to consume me burying his head

between my legs swallowing every drop of my juices, and most of the tricks he was doing with

his tongue made my clit tingle better than a vibrator on high with fresh batteries.

"Mmmmm, yes right there baby. I'm about to cum," I moaned out as I closed my eyes. As I was

about to climax I felt L.A. ram every inch of himself inside of me and just left it there. Not only did it feel like he was touching my stomach with how deep he threw himself inside of me, but that forceful motion caused me to squirt all over him.

"Come here," he said as he pulled me from the shower bench and pushed me against the

showers glass wall with my titties pressed up on the glass. I feel L.A.'s chunky dick slide inside of me before his fingers interlocked between mine, as he raised my arms above my head. As his chest rest against my back, I feel his strokes becoming more and more passionate and it was even more of a turn on feeling him suck, bite and kiss all over my back, shoulder and neck. With my body pinned between L.A. and this glass. I began to feel his dick harden up more inside of me and judging by his pace I can tell BIGGDADDY is getting ready to cum. As his strokes slow up, I turn my focus to contracting the lips of my pussy tighter around his stiffened shaft without completely cutting off all blood flow to his dick. In the process of trying to please him I ended up climaxing once more before he finally finished inside of me. When he came it was like a warm, small balloon bursting inside of me, and it felt amazing. When L.A. slowly eased himself out of me I turned around.

"I love you boy," I said in a soft tone as I placed my hands on his chin and my thumbs

caressed his cheek bones. L.A. gazed into my eyes as if I was the only thing in this world that mattered to him as he spoke.

"I love you too ma," L.A. responded as he reached past me grabbing the old spice body wash.

We took our time cleaning each other up and afterwards made our way to the bedroom. L.A.

and I laid in the bed, his head against my breast as I fondled through his beautiful locs and in that moment I knew that everything was going to be just fine.

As I slowly peeled open my eyelids the ray of sunlight piercing through the bedroom curtains

altered my vision for a slight moment. I then looked down at Monique as she laid peacefully on

my chest.

"Hey, wake up sleepy head," I whispered in her ear. I watched as she opened up her eyes and

looked up at me, and what started off as a beautiful smile on her face quickly became a look of

repulsiveness. Monique hopped out of the bed and ran as quickly as possible to the bathroom

and all I heard was sounds of regurgitation and bodily fluids dropping into the toilet. "You alright

in there baby?" I asked as I sat up in the bed trying to get a view from my side of the bed. Once

the vomiting stopped and the toilet flushed there was a brief moment of silence before Monique

appeared in the doorway of the bathroom.

"I'm good baby," she responded as she stood there brushing her teeth.

"Baby, I really think you need to go to the doctor and get checked out. This has been happening off and on for the past few weeks now?" I questioned as I climbed out of the bed making

my way over to the double vanity sinks to brush my teeth and wash my face.

"Yeah, but I'm fine honey," Monique calmly answered.

"Monique." I said as I looked over at her through the mirror.

"Okay, okay Frank I'll go in today. But I'm telling you now it's nothing. Just a waste of time," she

replied before hitting her mouth off with mouthwash.

"Thank you... You know I'd rather be safe than sorry. So, on another note whatchu got up for

today?" I asked as I finished up my morning ritual and walked back into the bedroom.

"I'm not sure honey. I don't have anything planned my best friend, Becca, wanted me to come

out with her this morning but I think I'ma just chill. I might go by my mom's later why what's

up?" she countered as she stood by the dresser lacing up her bra. As I sat down on the bed, I

noticed my phone on the nightstand beside me light up and when I picked it up to check it, it

was a text message from Janel that read...

"I just texted you to say hey! and to wish you a Happy Father's Day," with a picture of an

ultrasound below it. It hadn't even crossed my mind that today was Father's Day; but regardless, I don't have any children so why would she send me this. "Maybe it was just a group message," I thought to myself.

"Thanx but I'm not a father," I texted back before turning my attention back to Monique. "I

might make a few moves later but we ain't been out in a while, you trying to go out?" I asked.

"Yeah, we should go out tonight. What do you have in mind?" Monique questioned as she put

her hair in a bun.

"I'll leave it up to you baby. Whatever you want to do I gotchu," I responded as I put on my

white-T and tied down my dreads, then I felt my phone vibrate again.

"You will be," Janel responded back through text and as I read it, instant panic shot through my

soul.

"Okay I think I have something in mind," Monique replied with a huge grin on her face.

"Good, hey listen I gotta go," I said.

"What? Why what's up?" Monique asked as she walked towards the bed.

"Something just came up and I gotta go," I said as I walked over to my safe grabbed a few

stacks and tossed them on the bed before going on. "Here take this and go do a little shopping

with ya best friend and I'll meet you back here later tonight." I added as I continued to get

dressed.

"L.A., is everything okay?" she questioned as she took the money with a worried look on her

face.

"Yeah, baby everything is good, Jay-Money just hit me up and I gotta go take care of a few

Things, nothing big," I quickly responded as I got up and put on my shoes then grabbed my

jacket.

"Okay well, I guess I'll get dressed and give Becca a call to meet up with her. And I'll see you

tonight, right?" She asked as she walked me to the front door.

"Yep.... enjoy yourself.... And baby don't forget to ...."

"Stop by the doctor, I know, I know," Monique interrupted me and spat out before giving me a

kiss. I rushed to the car, got in, and drove off. As I was in the car, I tried to call Janel but it kept

going to her voice mail.

"Answer the fucking phone!" I yelled out. Now because of traffic it took me a little longer than usual to get to her house, but the whole drive there my mind was just racing. I hadn't seen

Janel or heard from her since the hospital situation and I didn't even cum inside of her so this has to be some kind of joke. I said to myself in utter disbelief of what was transpiring. After two

hours of traffic, I finally found myself pulling up to Janel's house," Fuck, I should have took the

god damn back road," I mumbled as I pulled into the driveway and hoped out then commenced

beating on the front door. I stood there for all of three minutes just banging on the door and

ringing the doorbell before Janel finally came to the door all calm.

"Hey." Janel said as she opened the door in nothing but a black sheer robe with matching bra

and panties. "Come in," She calmly added as she walked away from the front door leaving it

wide open.

"What was that text message all about?!" I asked in a very frustrated tone as I walked inside of

her house slamming the door behind me.

"I didn't want to be rude and not wish you a Happy Father's Day with today being Father's Day and all." She peacefully stated as she sat on the arm of the couch with her legs seductively crossed rubbing on her stomach.

"How can you? I didn't even cum inside of you the last time that we conducted business.

How do you even know it's mine? I haven't seen or heard from you in like two months?" I

questioned as I paced back and forth across the hardwood floors.

"Well, true you didn't finish last time, but remember that time before that? And I know because.... let's see I haven't fucked anybody but you since, you know, you killed my man,"

Janel responded very wisely as she slid down off the arm of the couch and flopped down in the

middle of it.

"How when you said you were on birth control?" I angrily questioned.

"Yeah, well I may have missed a few days of taking the pill," she quickly replied.

"Nah bitch! It don't work like that, you set me up," I shouted as I snatched her up off the couch.

"L.A. if I was you I would do two things. One remember that if anything happens to me, in

seventy-two hours your world will come crashing down and two take your muthafucking hands

off of me and watch your tone," Janel protested as she pulled away from me before going on. "

Now regardless of whether I set you up or not, what are you going to do? You're going to be a

father and that's that," she added.

"Janel how many months are you?" I asked as I sat down in the chair across from the couch

with pure disappointment on my face.

"Ah... about three months, give or take two weeks," she replied as she walked over to me and

sat down on my lap before continuing. "And I plan on keeping it just in case that's not clear. I

really hope it's a girl, don't you?" Janel added. My heart began to sink to the bottom of my

stomach. The thought of having a child by Janel was just sickening. This is where I draw the line.

"I can't. I can't do this anymore Janel. This done went on for long enough and it done went too

far! I'm done!" I said pushing her off my lap and onto the floor as I stood up and headed to
the door.
"What!? What am I not good enough to have your baby L.A.... Huh? Well guess what, I'm
having it so deal with it cause if you walk out of that door the video of you killing my boyfriend
and his dad that I recorded will go viral," Janel protested as she picked herself up off the floor.
"Thanks," I said as I pulled my phone from my pocket before going on. "See, I'm not sure why I
didn't think of this before" I added.
"What!?" she asked with a confused look on her face.
"Leverage." I simply responded.
"What leverage do you have?" she questioned.
"Well, now I have a recorded confession of you being at the scene of the crime and instead of
turning me in, you used the video as blackmail. Which by Michigan law makes you an
accessory to murder. Which makes leaking that video just as harmful to you as it is to me,"
I explained as I put my phone back into my pocket. Janel just stood there stuck in awe, and
because of her light skin tone, you could see the frustration all over her face she was just as red as she wanted to be. "Now what was it you were saying about walking out of this door? Cause
how I see it, if you take me down, you're coming too," I added and right as I turned to attempt to
open the front door, I felt a stunning blow to the back of my head. I felt myself falling then
everything went pitch black.

MEANWHILE.......
Bitch You Mad or Nah?

"Girl, I don't know what was so important this morning that made him just bust up like that. He
said one of his homeboys hit him up and he had to take care of some shit, but I don't know," I
said to Becca as we walked through the mall.
"I'm not sure either girl, but if you want me to call my P.I. just let me know. He does a good job
too," Becca responded.
"Bitch what the hell is a P.I. " I asked as we stopped inside of TjMaxx.
"A private investigator girl," she answered as she bit into a cinnamon roll she had gotten
from Starbucks.
"A private investigator? What do I need with a P.I.? And why do you have one?" I
questioned as we made our way over to the women's designer part of the store.
"Girl bye, whenever I get a gut feeling that Mark is out here doing something he ain't got no
business doing behind my back then I call my P.I. Eric. And he finds me the answers that I'm
looking for," Becca responded as she looked in the mirror holding a dress up to her body.
"So, Mark's been cheating on you?" I asked as I tossed a few articles of clothing into my cart.
"Oh God no, every time I have had Eric look into Mark and his fishy behavior he always comes
up empty. But you on the other hand, you already knew the lifestyle L.A. was living before y'all

started talking. I wouldn't be surprised if Eric found out that L.A. is creeping," Becca replied

as we continued to shop.

"First off L.A.'s not like that anymore. Secondly, I don't need a damn P.I. to follow my man

around. L.A. and I are an open book, if it was something that I wanted to know that badly I can

just ask him," I protested as we made our way to the dressing room.

"So, call him and ask him where he's at Mrs. Open book," Becca said in a very condescending

tone.

"You ain't said nothing but a word," I responded as I pulled my phone from my purse and

pressed speed dial two. L.A.'s phone just rang and rang so I hung up and tried again but nothing changed.

"What's wrong? No answer? See." she stated before she started to sing "Creep" by TLC.

"You know what Becca, whatever. You're just saying that because you never cared for L.A.

anyways," I responded as I tried on some of the clothes.

"You're right Monique I don't really care for L.A., but that's only because I don't think he's a good fit for you. I mean what do you see in him anyways. Next semester you'll be back in college for

your degree in Criminal Justice and he's still stuck being a thug like he's always been," Becca

said as she finished her cinnamon roll.

"You know what Becca stop! Just stop, because you being a real bitch. Just because you don't

see what I see in him don't mean we aren't a good fit. Clearly you must have saw something

in him at one point when you tried to holla at him."

"What!?" Becca blurted out interrupting me.

"Come on Becca don't play stupid he told me about how when I went off to college you tried to

get at him. And the crazy part is... you of all people knew that I liked L.A. and you still shot your

shot. You being my best friend and all I figured we was better than that, but I see some people

never change," I replied as I put back on my clothes and walked out of the dressing room.

" Monique, where are you going?" She asked.

"To mind my own damn business. I'm done here! And just so we're clear, the man that you

speak so poorly about, is my soon to be husband. So, I would really advise you to watch what

comes out of your mouth," I said as I walked off leaving Becca standing in the dressing area of

TjMaxx looking stupid. As I walked through the mall, I couldn't believe how bad she had my

blood boiling because I am not the type to get easily riled up. It was as if I couldn't control my

emotions. With Becca not glued to my hip anymore I continued my shopping grabbing a few

things for myself as well as L.A., if I saw something that I think he would look good in. I tried

giving L.A. a call once I finished up my little shopping before heading out to my car. But didn't

get an answer. As I went to get inside the car my phone began to ring.

"Hello.... Hey Ma," I said as I answered the phone.

"Hey Baby Girl, what you up to?" Mama questioned.

"Nothing much. I just finished a little shopping, why what's up? What are you up to young

Lady?" I asked as I pulled out of the parking lot.

"Well if you don't have any plans for today why don't you swing by for a little while?" Mama
suggested.

"I was actually planning on stopping by there today anyways since L.A. is out taking care of
some business," I stated.

"Oh, okay so when should I expect you?" Mama asked.

"Well, I'm on my way to my appointment now, and I don't see that taking no longer than an hour, so, I'll see you at about four," I answered.

"Alrighty then I'll see you at four. Stop by the store on your way and grab me a few apple
bites will ya," Mama stated in a question-like form but I know it was more like a demand.

"Yeah, Ma I got you. See you in a bit," I responded before we both hung up the phone. After
about another ten to fifteen minutes of driving I had finally arrived at ST. Johns. I parked
and walked through the revolving doors.

"Hi how are you? How can I help you?" the receptionist at the front desk asked as I
approached.

"Umm yes, I'm here for my appointment with Dr. Benson," I answered.

"Name please?" the young lady asked.

"Monique Mason," I responded as the short haired freckled face receptionist hit a few keys on
her computer.

"Ah-ha here you are. Alright well if you would just fill out this paperwork and take a seat in
the waiting area Dr. Benson should be with you shortly," the articulate and well mannered
receptionist said as she handed me a clipboard with paperwork to fill out. I took the clipboard

and filled in all of the needed information before returning the
clipboard and taking a seat in the
waiting area. After about a good ten minutes of waiting I finally heard
my name being called.
"Monique Mason," the middle-aged male nurse called out as he stood
to my far left in a doorway leading to a few examination rooms.
"That would be me," I said as I stood tall before making my way over to
him.
"Okay, well if you were to be so kind as to follow me right this way," he
responded as he took
the lead and walked me to the examination room four-seventy-three.
"You can just have a seat
right there," he added as he pointed over at the adjustable chair
stationed in the middle of the
room before going on. "I'm sorry for being rude, my name is Charles.
How are you doing today?" he asked as he sat down in the rolling stool
before rolling the blood pressure machine as well as himself over to the
side of me.
"Nice to meet you Charles, um do you know how long it will be before
I'm seen by Dr.
Benson?" I asked while removing my jacket.
"Honestly I'm not sure, but it shouldn't be long. Last time I saw him he
was finishing up with
someone else, but so that we have a head start I'm going to go ahead and
check out your
vitals. If you could give me your right arm I'll start with your blood
pressure," Charles replied
as he pulled apart the strap and wrapped it around my arm above my
elbow. "I'm sorry Monique I may be out of line with this comment, but
you are very beautiful," he added while pressing the
go button on the machine which started to apply pressure around my
arm.

"Thanks," I simply responded honestly at a loss for words.

"I'm sorry, I just had to put that out there. So, what brings you in today?" Charles questioned

after helping me to my feet and walking me over to the scale.

"Well actually I have been having really bad stomach pains and headaches," I answered as I

stepped onto the scale. Charles wrote down my weight and I walked back over to the adjustable chair and sat down.

"Stomach pains? huh? Any nausea?" he quickly asked as he nearly blinded me with the bright

beam of light, that came pouring from one of his tools he used to check my eyes and mouth.

"Yeah.... how'd you know?" I countered.

"Well, the symptoms that you are having are sometimes associated with someone who has a

peptic ulcer," Charles said as he documented my vitals.

"What's that?" I questioned with heightened worry in my voice as Charles took the

stethoscope from around his neck and placed one end into his ears and the other to my chest.

"Well peptic ulcers are scars in the lining of your stomach that may be the cause of your

abdominal discomfort. But those symptoms could be a magnitude of different things or it could

be nothing at all, that's for Dr. Benson to determine," he calmly reassured me. "But

hopefully everything is just fine. I'm finished up here, Dr. Benson should be with you shortly," Charles added as he walked out of the room and for the next two and a half hours, I sat in that

examination room playing Candy Crush on my phone. Right when I was starting to grow

impatient there was a knock at the door.

"Come in," I called out with a hint of irritation in my voice.

Back At Janel's Place

I know there's not many people who can relate, but as a man, your life flashes before your eyes feeling a cold piece of steel pressed up against your crotch.

"Whoa, whoa, whoa.... You ain't gotta do that Janel," I quickly responded.

"So, we have a clear understanding?" Janel asked as she pulled the pistol from my boxers and

waved it in front of me.

"Crystal clear.... Now can you untie me?" I questioned as she sat the gun back on the table

beside me.

"Nah..... Not just yet, I kinda like you being all tied up and me being in control. It's a bit of a

turn on if I may say so myself," she said as she climbed off of my lap and pulled my dick out of

my boxers as she slowly went to her knees. Janel slowly wrapped her warm lips around the

shaft of my dick and with a firm grip she slowly worked her way down it. As much as I tried to

fight off the erection, her soft and warm lips plus the constant rotation of her tongue made it

impossible for me to contain myself. Once she had topped me off to her liking Janel rose to her

feet, pulling her panties off to the side as she climbed on top of me and instantly, I felt the tight

moist grip from the lips of her pussy around the head of my dick. She let out a moan of relief as

she eased her way down harboring every inch of me inside of herself. Once Janel had finally fully mounted me, she started to rock back and forth as she bit, kissed , and licked all over my

neck and shoulders. The more rapid Janel's rocking became, the more I started to notice that

the screws that held down the chair were slowly separating from the floor.

"Damn baby, yes! Faster!" I called out in a very seductive tone leading her to believe that I was

enjoying myself, but really I was getting her to rock faster and harder to further loosen the

screws holding the chair down. After a few moments and multiple thrust from Janel rocking back and forth I felt the chair lift up higher, yet she didn't notice it.

"Mmmmmm ... FUCK!... L.A. I'm bouta cum.." Janel screamed out as she continued to vigorously ride me. As soon as Janel was getting ready to climax, I saw my opportunity to get free. Janel leaned forward and with every ounce of energy I could muster up I headbutted the shit out of her temple and like a tree she went sinking to the floor. Janel laid on the floor unconscious in front of me and without hesitation I began to rock back and forth in the chair, and before I knew it, I felt myself falling backwards. The back of the chair broke along with one of the legs causing the bondage around my wrist and ankles to loosen. Even though the fall kinda knocked the wind out of me I was still able to shake free and eventually I made it to my feet. Though I was winded I began to ineptly stumble out of the room, down the hall, and up a flight of stairs that lead into Janel's kitchen. As I made my way through the living room, I saw my pants and shirt draped over the arm of the couch. I swiftly threw on my clothes and without looking back I rushed to my car. I got inside of my car and drove straight home. Exceeding all speed limits, I made it there in less than twenty minutes. I hadn't noticed how dark and late it was outside until I pulled into my driveway. Instead of stopping in the middle of the driveway and going through the front door I pulled into the connected garage and went in the house through that door. I came in through the kitchen and the house was pitch black and when I attempted to cut on the lights there was two things I noticed. One being that the lights didn't work and two the sound of a gun racking back. It wasn't long before my eyes adjusted to the darkness, and I was able to see Janel standing there in the dining room with the pistol aimed at me.

"That wasn't nice," Janel said with ease. The kitchen wasn't one of the places where I usually

keep a gun so the playing field was definitely weighted in her favor, but I knew just how to even

it. I turned towards the back of the house and took off and as soon as I took off there was three

loud bangs and as I made it to the bedroom I collapsed. When I fell to the floor, I felt a sharp

burning in my chest and as I rolled over to my stomach attempting to crawl over to my

nightstand I couldn't help but notice my shortness in breath and blood trailing behind me. As my

breathing became scarce I had finally slithered over to the nightstand where one of my pistols

was stashed. and as I went to reach for the drawer handle I felt a striking blow to my ribs

which caused me to fall to my side and roll to my back. I looked up and Janel stood over me

with anger in her eyes and pistol in hand, because of her lighter skin tone the injuries that she

sustained from the headbutt was pretty gruesome. Her left eye was nearly swollen shut and I'm

assuming the fall to the ground is what broke her nose. And I may have caused that laceration to the right side of her face. "I promise you L.A. this never had to get to this point," Janel said as she stood over me pointing the gun down.

"No bitch you pushed it to this point when you decided to blackmail me and trick me into getting

you pregnant!" I replied with intense frustration as I felt my body weaken.

"No Frank, you brought all of this on yourself the moment you shot and killed my man. All over

money too I bet," she insinuated.

"Fuck you Janel, go to hell!" I responded as I hawked up blood and spit it in her face. She didn't

deserve an explanation as to why I killed Bossman, and I knew that's exactly what she was

fishing for.

"Nah, no thanks, I'll pass. We tried that arrangement already, remember? But what I won't do

is allow you to jeopardize the safety and wellbeing of me or my child. With that being said is

there anything else you would like to say!?" Janel asked.

"If you're looking for me to plead so that you will spare my life then you can just drop dead," I

said as my breathing became fainter, and I can feel my heartbeat begin to weaken. Right

after finishing that sentence, I heard four shots ring out and to my surprise none of them bullets

had my name on it. I opened up my eyes and watched as the gun and Janel fell to the floor.

In the doorway of the room stood Monique holding the blue steel twenty-two or better known as a Pocket Rocket that I had bought her a few weeks ago. Shaken up Monique rushed over to my

side stepping over Janel's lifeless body.

"Oh my God Frank.... Hey, hey, hey.... Honey look at me, look at me.... You're going to be just fine you hear me. I'm going to call the police.

They're going to send an ambulance and they're going to get you all patched up," Monique said as she pulled her phone from her pocket and

attempted to dial 9-1-1.

"No." I responded in a tranquil tone as I placed my hand on top of hers. "Don't ..." I added.

"Frank, what do you mean don't! You need medical help," she quickly replied.

"It's too late."

"Don't say that it's not too late. Baby, it's not," Monique interrupted me and said.

"Baby listen.... I'm good, I want you to know that regardless to what people may say about me

when I'm gone. Everything that I have done is because I love you. You are everything a man

could ever ask for. I never meant to cause you any hurt or pain. I love you Monique," I said as

my eyes began to close.

"I love you too L.A.," I heard Monique say as I felt a tear drop onto my cheek before my eyelids

shut and everything went silent.

(CREATE A BLANK PAGE FOR K.I.M. TO BE PUT IN LATER)

Like You'll Never See Me Again

"Damn Mo Mo what took you so long, miss I only have one stop to make?" My crazy mother
asked as she opened her front door letting me in.
"Ma, you wouldn't believe me if I told you," I replied as I walked in and took off my jacket.
"Humor me.... And did you grab my Apple Bites?" she questioned. After I hung up my jacket I
handed her the store bag I had brought in.
"So, tell me why after we got off the phone. I go to my appointment, and I was in the back
waiting in one of the examination rooms to be seen by my doctor for over TWO HOURS!
Two hours, I was so upset, and the worst part was I still didn't get seen. Not by the doctor
anyway," I responded as I followed her into the kitchen.
"What was your appointment for honey, if you don't mind me asking. And who did you get
seen by?" Mama Mason questioned.
"This male nurse named Charles was nice enough to keep me updated and once he realized
that my doctor was too tired to see me he went ahead and rescheduled me. But I had went in
to see about these stomach pains and headaches I have been having. Charles drew a sample
of blood so they can run a few tests and diagnose me properly," I simply answered.
"It might just be food poisoning. Was he cute?" she asked as she went in on her Apple Bite.
"Who?" I countered.

"The nice nurse, Charles, who kept you company," Mama replied with a grin on her face.

"Mom, stop," I stated.

"What? Girl you are engaged not married I believe it's okay to find another man handsome.

So, with that being said, was he cute?" she asked once again.

"Yes, mother, he was handsome. But on another note, what did your day consist of?" I

questioned.

"Nothing much. I'm still just getting used to being in this house all by myself. Hey and now

that you reminded me. Um, Becca called not too long ago and asked me if I had heard from you. And if I do, to tell you to give her a call," she stated as we made our way into the living room.

"Thanks for the message. But that phone call won't be happening," I responded.

"Why Mo what happened?" Mama asked. Now I don't typically like to get my mom involved

with my drama but since I can't get in touch with L.A., I need someone I can vent to.

"Well, ever since I came home from college and L.A. and I have been talking, Becca has had

nothing but negative things to say about L.A. And today while we were out, she decided to

once again be a Nasty Nancy about my relationship with L.A. I'm not sure what came over me

but I was fed up with it, so I told her about herself. This bitch had the audacity to say to me, "girl

I don't know what you see in him," and I told her, "clearly the same thing you saw." I explained.

"Hold on, wait? What you mean? L.A. and Becca used to mess around.?" she asked.

"Nah not like that, but L.A. told me that when I was away at college Becca tried to push up on
him. And he played her to the left, but still it's just the fact that she out of all people knew how I
felt about L.A. and she still went behind my back and tried to holla at him," I answered as I shot
L.A. a text message just checking in on him.
"Mo, you still ain't learned, huh?" she questioned.
"What do you mean Ma?" I countered.
"When you were a little girl, what did I always use to tell you about how to treat people?" my
mother asked.
"Treat people how I want to be treated. And that's exactly what I do Ma. What's there to
learn.?" I replied after glancing down at my phone noticing that there was still no response
from L.A., and honestly, I was starting to get worried.
"Right, but the part that you should have learned as you got older is don't expect people to treat
you the same way you treat them because if you expect people to treat you how you treat them, then you'll always bump heads with a person," she responded. As a little bell started to ring from the kitchen, "Oh that's the meatloaf," she added as she dashed to the kitchen. I pulled up my
dial pad on my phone and pressed speed dial two attempting to get in touch with L.A., but like
earlier I just got his voicemail. Not being able to get in touch with him was really starting to get to me because this is really not like him at all. Anytime L.A. would miss my call he would call back
or at least shoot me a text or something.
"Hey Ma, I think I'm going to hit the road," I said as I walked into the kitchen feeling in my gut

that something with L.A. was off.

"What.... but you just got here .... why are you leaving so soon?" Mama asked.

"L.A. just texted me, he made dinner reservations downtown at P.R.E.S.S. so I should get

home so I can freshen up and get dressed," I quickly lied. Luckily for me my mom was too busy

slicing meatloaf to look up at me as I spoke, because I have a little telltale sign for when I'm

lying my left eye twitches or so I'm told.

"Aw, well, if you say you have to go, I guess you have to go," she responded as she put down

the knife and walked over to give me a hug. "It's pretty dark out. Just do me a favor and text

me when you finally make it home. Okay?" Mama added as she walked me to the front door.

"I will do that my love," I responded as I grabbed my coat and gave her a kiss on the cheek.

"Oh.... tell L.A. I said hey," Mama called out from the doorway as I got Into my car. The whole

drive home I couldn't help but to think about why L.A. wouldn't be returning my calls or replying

to my text. My woman intuition was telling me that maybe he is out creeping, but at the same

time, I know that L.A. loves and respects me too much to disrespect me in such a foul way. Then I started to think about if he had jumped back into his old ways with selling dope but then again that wouldn't prevent him from reaching back out to me. Before I knew it, I was pulling up to L.A.'s house, once I pulled into the driveway the first thing that I noticed was L.A.'s garage door up, his car door cracked and the side door wide open. As I got out of the car, I heard three loud bangs then I saw a few sparks of light coming from the kitchen window where the loud bangs seemed to be coming from. Before gently closing my car door, I reached over into the center console and grabbed my blue steel twenty-two that L.A. had bought for me like a few days before the drive by, and I quietly made my way into the house. When I first walked in it took my eyes a moment to adjust to the complete darkness that filled the house. With my gun locked and loaded, I cleared the kitchen, living room and dining room. As I stepped into the hallway I could hear the sound of a woman talking yet I couldn't make out what was being said. I continued to walk down the hall heading to the master bedroom and the closer I got, the easier it was to make out what was being said.

"We tried that arrangement already! Remember? But what I won't do is allow you to jeopardize

the safety and wellbeing of me or my child.... with that being said is there anything else you

would like to say...?" the feminine voice mildly asked. As I leaned against the wall of the hall

right outside the bedroom door, I peeked my head inside and saw a woman standing there. She stood at the edge of the bed bare footed with just her bra and panties on pointing a gun down at L.A. who laid on the floor inches away from the nightstand where I know he keeps one of his

pistols. My heart began to race as I stepped into the room unseen by L.A. and unheard by the

woman, then I heard L.A.'s voice.

"If you're looking for me to plead that you spare my life then you can just drop dead," L.A. said,

and just like that I closed my eyes and let off four shots into the back of the half-naked woman.

When I opened my eyes, I watched as her lifeless body fell to the ground.

"Oh my God, Frank! Hey, hey, hey! Honey, look at me, look at me," I said after rushing to his

side and all shaken up. "You're going to be just fine you hear me? I'm going to call the police,
they're going to send an ambulance and they're going to get you all patched up," I added as I
propped his head up on my thigh while reaching in my back pocket and grabbed my phone then attempted to call 9-1-1.
"No," he responded in a tranquil tone as he placed his hand on top of mine. "Don't," he
added.
"Frank, what do you mean don't? You need medical help!" I quickly responded.
"It's too late," L.A. started to say before I cut in.
"Don't say that it's not too late! Baby, it's not!" I said as my eyes began to water up.
"Baby listen. I'm good, I want you to know that regardless to what people may say about me
when I'm gone. Everything that I have done, I did because I love you. You are everything a man
could ask for. I never meant to cause you any hurt or pain. I love you Monique," L.A. said to
me as his eyes began to close.
"I love you too L.A.," I said as tears dropped from my eyes down my cheeks and on to him. He
took one last gasp of air, then he was gone.
"Hello 9-1-1 what is your emergency?" the operator asked.
"I would like to report a murder," I answered.

As I woke up, I turned over and opened my eyes hoping that this was all just a dream, but it

wasn't. It was just another day of waking up to pain, heartbreak, and disbelief that the love of

my life was taken from me, and each day like today I wonder what if. Even though waking up to

this pain is excruciating, closing my eyes is even worse. Each time I close my eyes I have

nightmares or flashbacks of me killing Janel and watching as L.A. died in my arms. I had never

shot a person or anything for that matter let alone killed someone. So that guilt of knowing that I

took Janel's life weighs heavy on my heart. The police officers and detectives

told me that I did the right thing by calling and staying at the scene of the crime until they arrived because 'Protecting yourself is one thing but killing someone and running is another' one of

the airheads said like that was supposed to make me feel any better about the situation. It's crazy how just months apart from another, I've lost my dad, my brother, and now my fiancé and honestly I'm not sure how I'm going to make it. I dragged myself out of my bed brushed my teeth and washed my face and as I went to put my robe on, I heard the doorbell.

"Who is it?" I yelled out as I walked through the hall towards the door.

"It's Detective Davis. Can I speak with you?" the voice on the other side of the door

announced. I walked over and opened the door not too sure why Detective Davis needed to

speak with me.

"How can I help you Detective?" I asked as I stood in the doorway.

"Monique let me start by saying that I am really sorry for your loss. How are you holding up? I

Just left Mrs. King's house and she wasn't doing too well," Detective Davis said as he just stood

there holding his phone and tablet.

"I'm holding up. I'm sorry not to be rude or anything but why are you here? Did they assign

you to his case or something?" I questioned as I folded my arms across my chest.

"No, actually I came across some new information in regard to your brother's case that gave

me a hit on who the killer is. May I come in?" he asked. I stepped to the side and Detective

Davis removed his hat as he entered my home.

"What new information?" I asked as we walked into the dining room and sat down at the

table across from each other.

"Did you know that L.A. was a drug dealer?" Detective Davis asked simply ignoring my

question.

"I'm sorry, but what does that have to do with my father and brother's case?" I countered.

"I have reason to believe that your brother's case and this one are connected. So, did you or didn't you know that L.A. was a drug dealer?" he questioned once more.

"I don't have to answer any of your questions, Detective, especially without my lawyer present.

But what I can do is ask you to get the hell out of my house!" I demanded as I stood up pointing

in the direction of the door.

"I came here in the comfort of your home to simply ask you a few questions. But if that's the route that you want to go then I'm going to have to ask you to turn around and put your hands

behind your back," Detective Davis said as he stood up pulling out his cuffs.

"What? Why? What did I do!?" I asked but he just ignored me.

"You have the right to remain silent, anything you say can and will be used against you in the

court of law. You have the right to an attorney if you cannot afford one, then one will be

appointed to you," he said as he walked around the table to my side.

"Okay, okay. Stop! what are you arresting me for?" I asked.

"Felony obstruction, since you don't want to answer my questions here maybe you'll be more

inclined to answer them down at the station. After processing and booking you'll most likely sit in a cell for a few hours before talking to me again but at least then your lawyer will be there.

With today being Saturday, you're not seeing a judge until Monday, which means you won't be able to post bail until Tuesday night," Detective Davis made it very clear as he turned me towards the wall and locked the cuff on my left wrist. "This could have all been avoided had you just answered my questions," he added.

"Okay, okay, I'm sorry I have just been dealing with a lot of different emotions. I'll answer

your questions just please don't take me to jail. Whatever you want to know I'll try to the best of

my abilities to answer them," I pleaded as tears began to fall from my eyes.

"Are you sure you're willing to cooperate?" He asked as I felt the grip of the cuffs around my

wrists loosen.

"Yes.... yes.." I answered.

"So, I'm assuming you knew L.A. was in fact a drug dealer?" Davis asked in more of a
statement form after removing the cuffs and taking a seat.
"Yes.... I knew he sold drugs, but after we got engaged, he promised me he was giving up that
lifestyle," I answered.
"And when was this?" he quickly questioned.
"Ah.... January seventh," I replied.
"And you don't find it strange that two days before your proposal your brother's body was found
burned beyond recognition in the trunk of a car next to your father?" Detective Davis
responded.
"Exactly what are you getting at Detective?" I sat back and questioned.
"Well, what I'm getting at is the fact that you knew L.A. was a drug dealer, your brother sold
drugs and hell your father was their supplier. And out of all three of them L.A. is the only one
that didn't die," he stated.
"I'm sorry?" I simply responded.
"Come on Monique, what was it about? the money? Did daddy stop paying for your college
tuition? Or was it not supposed to go down like that? Was L.A. just supposed to take the
money and split it with you? But let me guess you started to get greedy and L.A. started
dipping back into his old ways with the ladies? You come home find him in the bed with your
brother's ex and you thought to yourself that this would be a perfect time to get rid of the middle
man?" Detective Davis ranted on as I just looked in awe and utter disbelief of all the lies

coming out of his mouth.

"You honestly have the balls to walk into my house and throw false allegations at me about my

husband after he just died in my arms not even a full three days ago!" I said in a very

acrimonious manner. There was a moment of silence as Detective Davis fiercely gazed into my

eyes.

"You honestly had no idea?" he said with a hint of confusion in his voice as he played around

with his tablet before going on. "This morning I received an email from a fake yahoo account

and attached to the email was this video. "He added as he sat the tablet on the table and slid it

over to me. I picked up the tablet and pressed play, as I watched the video I saw my brother

helping someone carry my dad to the trunk.

"What is this?!" I questioned.

"Keep your eyes on the screen" he responded, by the time I looked back down the guy that was

helping James carry our father to the car and put him in the trunk was walking back towards

James with a gas canister in hand. The guy started to pour gas all over the body in the trunk

but stopped when James reached in the trunk and grabbed something. Once James turned

around to the guy who was pouring the gas I heard a gunshot. I saw James slump over onto the edge of the trunk looking as if he was begging for his life. Then the man with the gas shot him

again, and James' body fell over into the trunk beside our dad. The guy finished pouring the

gas into the trunk and as he turned around...

"Oh.... my....God..." I said as the tablet slipped from my hands and onto the table. "I think

I'm going to be sick," I added as I ran over to the kitchen sink. "I didn't just see what I thought

I saw, did I?" I asked after I was done throwing up but still hunched over the kitchen sink.

"I know this is the last thing that you thought you would ever hear. But yes, L.A. murdered your

father and brother," Detective Davis answered. And as those words came from his mouth, my

insides continued to come out of my mouth. "Excuse me," I said as I walked past Detective Davis after hearing my phone ring. "Hello?"
I said in a weak voice as I answered the phone.

"Hello, this is Charles from St. John's is this Monique Mason that I'm speaking with?" he
asked.

"This is her," I said as I slowly walked back into the kitchen.

"Okay, I'm sorry for verification purposes could you please tell me your date of birth and the last

four of your social?" Charles asked.

"May twenty-first, ninety-five.... And the last four of my social is twenty-three fourteen. I'm

sorry Charles for being rude but if you could just say what you called to say that would be great

because this really isn't a good time," I explained.

"Not a problem. Well, you know that we took some blood from you three days ago, when you

were here to run some tests and your results came back today," he said before going silent.

"So, what's wrong with me Charles? Is it something life threatening?" I asked.

"No..... it's more like life changing," Charles answered.

"What? What do you mean?" I questioned.

"I'm not sure how simple you want me to put it Monique but you're pregnant. Actually, a little

under three months. I'm surprised that you're just now showing symptoms," he replied. As that

eight letter word rolled off of his tongue my eyes widened, and my heart felt like it sank to my

feet....

"Pregnant?"

(CREATE A BLANK PAGE FOR K.I.M. TO BE PUT IN LATER...)..

THE END

(THE FOLLOWING IS THE SYNOPSIS/THE SHORT
OVERVIEW OF THE BOOK ON THE
BACK OF THE BOOK)

E.S.C.A.P.E.
Eventually Sex will Cripple A Person's Emotions

In his efforts to E.S.C.A.P.E., L.A. has found the love that his heart always desired, but it came at a cost. After finding out who murdered his father and avenging his death, L.A. struggles with his own bag of secrets. Guilt consumes his thoughts and dreams while a woman with leverage
threatens to jeopardize his relationship as well as his freedom. L.A. has given up the lifestyle he
was so prone to living for a type of love he had never encountered before. Now he is faced with
a choice: either expose his secrets and risk losing the woman of his dreams and his freedom
or live by the rules and regulations set forth by the "Devil!" Even though L.A. made it out of the
streets and tried to change his life around for the better, he ended up falling victim to something
far worse. Blackmail. This sudden shift of direction in his life caused him to question if he was
just a bad guy pretending to be good or a good guy just pretending to be bad? Blackmail, lies,
scandal, sex and love make up about 95 percent of this book. The other 5 percent
is the deception and secrets L.A. is willing to take to his grave. Too bad technology would not
allow his secrets to die with him.

About the Author

"Whats good, you miss me?

I apologize fa wait; but in publishing my story ah new chapter surprisingly arose. I gotta beautiful daugter named Reagan you guys, but ya'll family so please call her TeaCup. Nothing after this gone top that bundle of joy, so instead ill just let you know what she motivated me to do. My team and I scratched tooth and nail to open up our online store front where you can find some of ya most TOXIC apparel. As well as launching our website for TheeEdibleTeddyBear where you'll be sure to find a new favorite EXOTIC adult treats to aid in your "uplifting" process. BUT wait theres more, to close out the year [B.B.T] Bodie By Teddy will be available for purchase soon. One of many to come from Teddy's aromas."

Read more at https://linktr.ee/theeedibleshop.